Shelter of Daylight
July 2024

Short Stories

Poetry

Illustrations

*

THE STAFF OF SHELTER OF DAYLIGHT:

MANAGING EDITOR: Tyree Campbell
WEBMASTER: David Blalock

Cover art "Starry Night" by Richard E. Schell
Cover design by Laura Givens

Vol. V, No. 2   July 2024

A Little Help, Please

In the world of the small indie press we fight a never-ending battle for attention to our work, as writers and in publishing. Here's an example: big publishers [you know who they are] have gobs of $$$ that they can devote to advertising and marketing. Here at Hiraeth Publishing, our advertising budget consists of the deposits for whatever soda bottles and aluminum cans we can find alongside the highways. Anti-littering laws make our task even more difficult . . . ☺

That's where YOU come in. YOU are our best promoter. YOU are the one who can tell others about us. Just send 'em to our website, tell them about our store. That's all. Just that.

Of course, we don't mind if you talk us up. We're pretty good, you know. We have some award-winning and award-nominated writers and artists, plus other voices well-deserving to be heard [not everyone wins awards, right?] but our publications are read-worthy nevertheless.

That number once again is:
www.hiraethsffh.com
Friend us on Facebook at Hiraeth Publish
Follow us on Twitter at
@ HiraethPublish1

New from Hiraeth Publishing!!

Starwinders:

Nohana's Heart

The scion of a corporate hierarch, Angrboda Vigdisdottir (Ayvy) wants to hijack a gold shipment to prevent an interstellar war. Disgraced security operative Pol Cahill is the ideal partner for her, given his skill set. Unfortunately, personalities clash. Finally, on a remote world, the two encounter one another in a tavern, and find that a young woman named Nohana, intensely educated and with a desire to travel among the stars, takes to the pair.

But the personalities continue to clash even as plans are laid to steal the gold. Nohana fills the power vacuum and becomes the so-called adult in the room. But Cahill is shot and wounded before they can carry out their plan. Nohana now has no choice but to try to save the day, despite her lack of experience. Meanwhile, the war awaits.

Ordering links:
Print: https://www.hiraethsffh.com/product-page/starwinders-nohana-s-heart-by-tyree-campbell

PDF: https://www.hiraethsffh.com/product-page/starwinders-1-nohana-s-heart-by-tyree-campbell

ePub: https://www.hiraethsffh.com/product-page/starwinders-1-nohana-s-heart-by-tyree-campbell-1

For younger readers ages 9 to 90!
Pyra and the Tektites!

Pyra, age thirteen, is running away from home in the Asteroid Belt because she's not doing well in school. Her parents want to send her to Mars for school, and she doesn't want to go. She sneaks aboard a cargo shuttle, and falls asleep in the hold. When she awakens, she finds herself in free-fall; the shuttle has been seized by the Tektites, a group of rebel pirates.

. . . and the adventures begin!

This volume encompasses the first three novellas: Aquarium in Space; The Unicorn Stone; Smugglers!

Print: https://www.hiraethsffh.com/product-page/pyra-and-the-tektites-by-tyree-campbell

Reflections on the Other Side

Sandra Siegienski

The glassblower glided through the island marketplace, her grace drawing the notice of the mirror-spirit once again. Such a melding of soul and dignity as hers he hadn't seen anywhere in all his centuries, and a place in his mirror-heart warmed and strengthened. And, once again, he yearned to reach out to her.

A playful exuberance filled her stride as she approached his frame, crossing from the artists' studio across the pathway, her face reflecting an intense thoughtfulness along with a hint of the kind of love that arises from sharing beloved poetry and song. Her hat crowned hair the deep glossy brown of koa wood—one of those straw hats pretending to be a fedora, with a yellow hibiscus seated in the hatband: a moment of sunshine over sarong and coral-toned shirt. The brilliant flower lent her especial joy.

Her gaze touched his mirror. And he hoped....

The moment, like so many before, defined his mirrored existence.

Interestingly, his world of *mirror* hadn't been easy for him to discern, at first. The truth of his limited dimensions had fallen upon him by degrees, across an expanse of time that he came to understand only by the many tides of people streaming by, in place after place in which his frame rested. Through those people's lives, he'd gained an understanding of their worlds, hopes, fears, and motivations as their civilizations changed.

Over the ages, he'd seen all manner of human conditions: plagues, famines, mad political upheavals, tragic romances, drunken brawls, and much in between— for mirrors lay witness to all, although few people noticed what lay beneath their surfaces. The full truth of his contained presence hit home the day a mirror was set opposite him, reflecting mirror after mirror, disappearing into eternity; he was destined to merely view a domain of people unlimited by frames, their outside-mirror world running parallel to his inside-mirror world, the distinct disconnection between the two proving so difficult to bridge.

But today, the glassblower's arms cradled a bouquet of gardenias, which in turn sheltered a whimsical curve of fluted blown glass. A fine strand of Ni'ihau shells shone like pearl against the bronze skin of her neck, while a few dark burns graced her arms—hallmarks of her trade.

Wishing—as always—not to be restricted by his less-than-her-dimensional existence, he willed his mirror essence against the glass, against that ultimate division between reflection and human life. The magnitude of his effort caused a tremor in his ornate gilt-trimmed frame this time, freeing several flecks of fine golden paint, which drifted to the steppingstones before her sandaled feet, reflecting daylight in a burst of sun-glitter.

At seeing the minute starfield in her path, she slowed, glancing up to his mirror, touched and bemused.

Her gaze lit a spark in his heart—a star shining stronger than any in the sky. For the first time, he'd touched life beyond the mirrored world.

A petal dropped from the gardenia, falling to rest amid the gold. Then, after a thoughtful tilt of her head, the artist passed by with a graceful swish of sarong and a disappearing curved heel: a shadow of a figure moving with three-dimensional ease.

She was gone.

But she'd smiled, and seen beyond her reflection.

*   *   *

A week passed, perhaps two or ten—time passed strangely within the realm of mirrors—as he waited for the glassblower to reappear, searching for that distinctive face and flicker of understanding humor in her eyes, and her hat-crown with its blossom of joy. Time had taught him patience, but the slow crawl of each minute as the sun moved from ocean horizon to mountainside grew difficult to bear. So did the dark passage of star-filled nights, with indifferent windows surrounding the gallery, and only the soft *shush* of distant waves giving him companionship.

Arbitrarily, he marked days by sunsets and minutes by the grand clock tower across the marketplace.

His beveled glass had moved to this outdoor gallery a few years earlier, resting beside a walkway traversed by a multitude of preoccupied people on myriads of errands: all bright shirts and sunglasses and bicycles, under the lacey shade of koa trees. Alone, with no other nearby mirror to travel to, he'd occupied himself with a little mischief: creating foggy mists that obscured reflections and couldn't be wiped away (an ability gained from emulating morning mists seeping over pathways). Without warning, he'd swiftly clear the glass, and the sudden appearance of a passersby's reflection caused them more than a little surprise. Some viewed themselves with laughter, others with unexpected clarity or a frown. Some peered coyly at themselves. Others merely blinked. On one such day, the glassblower had first passed by, with her face turned towards the clouds and rain. The insightful kindness in her eyes had created an unexpected yearning in himself...a yearning for something of depth, far beyond his frameworld. It had lingered.

One midsummer evening the artist reappeared, her azure pareu capturing the color of the sea, her wisteria bag weighted with diminutive glass sculptures. An emerald hummingbird darted at her hat—now crowned by plumeria —making her laugh. She was filled with life and happiness, on the cusp of middle-age yet undiminished by cares and worry. Silvery lace graced her bronze shoulders. A gold pendant nestled between her collarbones. *Celina*, the tiny golden letters told him.

Celina.

He imagined moving his lips in silent mirror-words, imagined stepping into her world: with no wall of beveled glass separating them, that eternal boundary of *mirror*. He wished for hands that could touch the glass near her introspective face.

Today, she paused before her reflection, studying herself as if searching for something she expected—or desired—to find. "Sometimes, I think I see...." Her voice trailed away.

See...*what?*

"...your spirit."

9

Sudden hope flared, filling him.

He quickly sent across his glass an image of rolling fog, billowing playfully here and there, nestling into frame corners in the shapes of maile and bougainvillea like those adorning the walkways. Celina traced the fine curves of blooms with her fingertips, as a dim rumble grew behind her. A motorcycle roared by, the machine's silver skin reflecting the streetlamps...so unlike the quiet carts and horses that had once filled the world's roadways. The mechanical roar shook his frame.

Celina turned away, distracted, the moment broken, her world again separated from his beveled realm.

With substantial effort, he shifted his angle just enough to reflect the glow of a streetlamp onto her path, lighting her way down the dimming lane. She glanced from path of light to him and smiled—a smile signaling an undefined understanding of the mysteries of alternative existences.

A touch of sweet sadness mingled with his new joy, a spot of brightness he couldn't contain, a life of its own. *It must be...love.*

"Goodnight, and thank you," Celina whispered, walking onward but slowly, as if she wished to linger but couldn't. "I'd like to meet again." And she vanished once more into her outside-mirror-life while he savored mixed joy and sorrow.

* * *

Over the ages, he'd often observed the solemn touch of loneliness in others and wondered about the longing and sadness it caused.

Now he knew.

His life hadn't always been so isolated. People had routinely moved his mirrors to new places: a tavern, a country mansion, a gallery. He himself moved with relative ease between mirrors of close proximity; the realms of all mirrors were mysteriously interconnected. He preferred long stretches within palaces or curvatures of ballrooms, for they were less limiting. An eternity in mirrordom was easier to drift through when people danced joyfully around him.

Even so, he'd begun grieving his invisibility in the eyes of others who saw only their own reflections...and never him.

Celina, with her thoughtful laughter, had changed that.

But what had she seen?

Intrigued, he began creating a true image for himself from his mirror-fog: a face with eyes kind and true, hands giving and gentle, a pleasing body clothed in colors that complemented hers. The playful tilt of a stylish cap. An image to reach beyond the frameworld holding him in.

As his image grew less mist-obscured, pedestrians glanced at him in vaguely uncertain curiosity, their gazes lingering on his image for an extra second, looking back over their shoulders as they passed.

Timing was critical. Once, his too-sudden appearance created a shrieking rush of unwanted attention, forcing him to hide until the fervor died down.

One morning, when no one was around, he displayed his image with all his strength.

"You've got it," said a mirror-voice of close proximity, startling him. "You're a solid image. Well done!"

Astonished, he asked, "Who are you?" in the silent language of his kind.

"A traveler, much like yourself."

Like myself?

Amid his recent distractions, a new mirror had been set at an angle to his. In it, a presence exuded an obscure aura holding no greater clarity than his own image. Thrilled to meet another of mirrordom for the first time, he asked, "Are there many others like us? How did you find me, here?"

"I'm afraid it was pure chance. Few of us exist, to my knowledge, but if you search long enough you'll find them."

"Are they...what do they....?" He couldn't finish.

A sigh. "Some are unaware, mercifully. Others, like yourself, are only too aware."

He thought. "Do they try to take shape? Can they?"

"Yes. Some do. Some even try to leave."

"Leave," he echoed. A new idea.

"Yes. But it's as difficult as it sounds. I've met no one successful, of course, although legend tells us of possibilities otherwise." A heavy sigh. "I'm afraid I no longer quite have the heart to believe the legends."

Hope was rising in him like a crescendo, anyway. "You've pursued outside life?"

"Once you're aware, you can't help but try. And so, I did. You've tried, yes? To leave the mirror realm?"

"I have."

A weighted pause followed. "I'm sorry. We all fail, yet —"

"All? There must be a way." He couldn't imagine this inventive world being without an answer.

"Maybe. Every so often the mirror-realm gives someone a chance, I've heard, if their desire is true and strong enough. Another legend, perhaps, but one can hope."

It sounded like an exercise in painful, baited waiting. He shook his image-head for the first time. "I will keep trying."

"As you wish," the visitor said, aggrieved. "It's your choice. But look to your future as well."

In his future, he saw an eternity of mirrored lifetime. The glimpse of legend gave him hope—perhaps ill-fated, but hope all the same. He had to admit he'd seen nothing either leave or enter a mirror, although he *had* shaken flecks of golden paint free from the frame. Maybe it was possible. Maybe.... "For how many centuries have I believed I was truly alone?" he whispered.

"More than enough. It's difficult, in this realm," his visitor said, with sympathy. "To gain anything, we must travel often, and that's dangerous. Make the wrong move, and you get trapped for decades. That happened to me. And you—you're in a risky place here. Too isolated."

How well he knew that. "But traveling is still worth it to you?"

A soft chuckle. "I outgrew every other desire. I no longer fear exploration, nor its consequences."

"How long have you lived?

A moment of quiet passed. "I leave you to your future," his visitor replied instead. Soon, a worker came by and lifted the frame away—and his chance to shift to a new mirror was vanishing. But Celina was here.

Leave, though. Could he really leave his mirror? For perhaps forever? He searched quickly for more questions, finding none he wished to hear answers for, and could only say with heartfelt appreciation, "I wish you the greatest success in all your explorations."

"I reach outward. Always outward." Wistful, the voice drifted away.

"Wait!" he called suddenly. "Tell me about love!"

But his visitor was gone.

*   *   *

His one experience with love had happened in a faraway countryside, long ago.

He'd gazed upon the saddened eyes of a weeping girl as she'd lingered before his mirror, folding and refolding a silk handkerchief embroidered with initials of midnight blue, a pretentious ring glittering on her finger.

He'd never before approached her private rooms—he was no voyeur, in either human or mirror terms—but her distress made him linger at her wardrobe, worried. She'd stared into her reflection as if envisioning someone else, then leaned forward and kissed the glass.

Yearning to give what she so greatly desired, he instinctively leaned forward in a shared kiss, just as an ostentatiously dressed young man wearing an equally pretentious ring burst into the room. Seeing the girl, he'd laughed—a derisive bark designed to cut to the quick. The gentle spell broken, she'd clenched her silk handkerchief, her sensitive face burning with humiliated misery.

Outraged in her defense, his mirror-spirit instinctively reached outward to erase the derision filling the young suitor's face, but a new blow fell in force upon him instead: He could not leave his mirror.

The girl fled.

Her suitor followed.

Wishing only to comfort her, he'd waited for hours. She did not reappear.

In coming days, the girl and suitor separated to different lives amid angry words. The pretentious ring was returned, the house closed up. His mirror was moved to a gallery.

Ages passed after that shared kiss. He shifted from mirror to mirror, searching public walkways, seeking the girl, examining all faces for her likeness. He never found her, but the idea of love inspired him: that intimacy shared in a touch, a glance, a breath. Lips to touch and kiss, even if separated by glass.

With curiosity, he listened to all who spoke of love, but it eluded him.

*　*　*

Celina appeared on an autumn morning in the near-empty marketplace, approaching him with spritely elegance, the folds of her tangerine pareu swishing against long legs in stylish poise. A gardenia lay tucked atop her bag. The mellow brown of her skin had deepened in the full sun of summer.

With a twinkle of gentle humor, she eyed her reflection, giving him a sideways smile as if to say, *Ah—I am here. We are right where we're supposed to be.*

Now, he thought, reaching outward to his limits, willing his image to appear in folds of fog, and his fingertips to touch where hers had. Barely daring to hope, he saw her attention focus...not on her reflection, but squarely upon *him.*

Glancing around, she removed her hat and leaned to gently touch her forehead against the glass, against his fingertips. "I see you, with more than my eyes," she whispered, stunning him into immobility. "I've been waiting for the right time to tell you."

Voices sounded behind her. She quickly pretended to adjust her attire—although he recognized she was no longer observing just herself—and, lowering her eyes, she said, "I'll visit again," and walked past. Her image sparkled in windows across the way, the trees framing her like kahilis: royal standards honoring her depth of insight. Looking thoughtfully back toward him, she turned the corner.

Who was this woman, and of what nature, that she could understand him?

Night fell. Darkness came, then light returned. Sunrise bloomed, color saturating the world anew. Another day.

To his joy, over the coming weeks and months, Celina began to appear often, sometimes in a bright sarong, sometimes a rain-spattered coat—whatever suited the capricious weather. Each time they met, he brought forth the best of himself: an expression of kindness, a gesture of love, a nod of hope. He learned to subtly shift his angle, lighting her way when the evenings grew dark. He reflected sunlight to shrubs adorning shadowy corners of the marketplace, keeping the jasmine blooming far heavier than usual, so she could cherish the sweet scent. He learned to mimic movements of speech, trying to convey his thoughts to her as she could to him.

Sometimes she spoke; sometimes they shared only a companionable silence amid mutual gazes of growing love and trust. "Perhaps the legends are true," she once whispered.

His curiosity roused, he tried to find a way to ask what legends she'd heard—and what she meant—while wishing he could share his. He failed, but redoubled his efforts to be visible, to move and speak like her.

Often, she arrived at first light of dawn. At midday, sun-shadows lay small around her sandaled feet. At sunset, sky colors of coral and magenta glimmered across her heavy hair.

"I see you best in the morning," she told him, her fingertips touching his image. "You are my morning star."

He moved his lips in the soundless shapes of words he couldn't voice. "You are my everything star."

She brought her own touches of enchantment to his world—quoting phrases of poetry, telling a story, singing a bit of song or chant, or leaving a bright-colored blossom of glass where he could see it. Sometimes, she left a handwritten note where he could read it, before rain washed away the ink or wind scattered the paper.

Although he could read many scripts, the fine ability to form his mirror-mist into delicate letters with which to reply eluded him. One day for her, he carefully formed *A-R-*

T upon his glass, letting the shapes dissipate before anyone else saw.

Celina's eyes glistened. "Glass is a window to many things, if you can only understand its ways," she said. "I learn from the Old Masters, and hope to gain their skills soon." She rested her gentle hand against his frame until an arriving exuberant wedding group forced her to move away.

They couldn't linger together long; not in the everlasting stream of passersby, and she had no means to purchase or move his heavy mirror. So, they lived day-to-day, in sparkling moments of glimmers of joy, or a look, or a sigh. Small things.

He never ceased trying to leave his mirror. Celina only said softly, "Someday, we'll find an answer. In the meantime, we must enjoy all we have."

He listened, but held onto his hopes.

One day, he noticed against her sundress a pin the shape of a tiny red heart and torch. That day, her gaze lowered away from his. "I may go on a journey, someday," she told him, her voice low. "But I'll always be with you, in my own way."

"What do you mean? When?" he tried to question, but his manner of speech was not yet successful, nor could he form sufficient words in mirror-mist.

"Not for a while," she only answered. She said no more about it, but from then on, her jovial walk grew a little slower, her pace more methodical, then laborious. Her skin paled. Her body grew thinner, her steps heavier. The light in her eyes dwindled. Sometimes, she fleetingly touched her hand to her chest.

He worried.

His signs of loving concern she deflected with a pensive, wistful tilt of her head. "Don't worry. I'll always find my way back." She touched her fingers to his mirrored lips, leaning her warmth against his glass.

She spent more and more time in the glassworks studio, emerging after long nights and long days, lost deep in thought. The day came when heavy darkness colored the skin beneath her eyes, and her fingertips tinged blue. With a chill, he recalled seeing these signs through the ages... and how they invariably led to death.

Again, she leaned against his frame and he exulted in her touch, although fear filled him that her presence might soon no longer touch his life. "I see you," she whispered. "You are always here."

He couldn't let her lose her joy. He pressed at the barrier between them, trying—forever trying—for a true voice. "Always."

She seemed to hear, and sighed.

After that evening, several weeks passed without her presence. To him, the passage of time slowed to interminable infinity.

*　*　*

Celina appeared as the last of sunset diminished into the blue hour, her skin seeming thin to translucence, her breathing labored. "I had to see you," she whispered, sinking to the ground before his mirror, while he knelt his image as close to her as he could, helpless.

Rain pattered the sidewalks. No one lingered today in the damp and darkness to intrude.

"I love you." His mouth moved in the shape of words he'd heard so many times—but the first time he'd said them himself. "You bring my world alive."

She smiled, her brown eyes warm. "I'm so tired." Her voice dimmed, her breathing growing softer. Her eyes closed and she drifted to sleep, leaning against his frame, her body embracing the glass.

A moment later, her chest ceased rising and falling. Frantic, he scanned the streets, seeing only Night. No one to help.

Celina's body lay still.

No. Beseeching, he reached for her, seeking any sign of that sweet life within her, so far out of reach.

Celina!

No. *No. NO.* He shoved his glass. The frame shook and groaned. Reflections of lamps and stars and moon danced across the warping surface.

He'd already lived an eternity and couldn't imagine another without her, his everything star, or a world in which she no longer existed. Submerged in anguish, he chose his fate—to stay here, alone, forever. To remember every moment of hers. To preserve her memory in eternal isolation, never to love another, if that's what hope and love and legend required of him. He would stay.

Then, his fingers touched fabric.

Warmth sang through him, not from beyond the mirror, but from a gentle aura touching his spirit. He turned from the outside world to the sudden sense of *presence* within his mirrordom.

Beside him stood Celina, surrounded by fine mist, gazing into his eyes.

"You're here," he whispered, reaching disbelieving fingertips toward her gentle face. His words were clumsy, yet reflections of a thousand joys appeared in her brown eyes. "You're here."

She cast a long look at her body, her shell lying at rest before his mirror, and gave a smile that outshone a thousand small suns. "Always," she whispered. "I'm right where I'm supposed to be."

From Sea To Land
by Denny Marshall

The Thursday Child
A Yoelin Thibbony Rescue
By Tyree Campbell

Yoelin Thibbony performs Rescues of children, people, and articles, sometimes for a fee, sometimes for free. But she has begun to doubt her own identity; her childhood memories of abuse and slavery are starting to make less sense to her. Now, events tumble around her. A former lover who betrayed her has been killed, and the authorities are looking for her. His three-year-old son has been brought to Yoelin by a mysterious woman with an even more serious agenda; their spaceship is blown up at the Spaceport. Yoelin, unwilling to abandon a child in need of a Rescue, must follow a line of investigation that leads her into her own dubious past, and to a vast and secret conspiracy —a long game—that threatens the lives of the people she cares about most. This time, the confrontation is one that almost certainly she cannot win.

But when did that ever stop her?

https://www.hiraethsffh.com/product-page/Thursday-child-by-tyree-campbell

Whispers from the Intoxicating Abyss

By Lee Clark Zumpe

You may not realize it, but they're out there: impossible shadows, omniscient horrors, and unseen, unknowable entities scattered across the great gulfs of nothingness at the edges of the universe. In this collection, author Lee Clark Zumpe draws back the curtain from the invisible realm, divulging its arcane secrets and ghastly revelations. Come walk paths meandering over shunned worlds adrift in darkness, and through seemingly mundane, liminal spaces that might be overrun with ancient shadows at any moment.

Stories are inspired by the works of H. P. Lovecraft.

Type: Collection of Short Stories
Cover price: Print: $13.95; ePub: $3.99; PDF: $3.99
Ordering links:
Print: https://www.hiraethsffh.com/product-page/whispers-from-the-intoxicating-abyss-by-lee-clark-zumpe

ePub: https://www.hiraethsffh.com/product-page/whispers-from-the-intoxicating-abyss-by-lee-clark-zumpe-2

PDF: https://www.hiraethsffh.com/product-page/whispers-from-the-intoxicating-abyss-by-lee-clark-zumpe-1

Seen in Green and Orange
F.P. Wilson

Joe grinned, sat back, and closed his eyes. His head rocked as he listened to the roar and screech of the 1-train. It clattered its way down the island, following grimy tracks that carried it through Manhattanville, Harlem, and the Upper West Side. The plastic subway seat beneath him would be his gum-bottomed home for another half an hour. He smiled, thinking that despite his *incredible* powers, it would still take him forty-five minutes to reach his destination.

He'd often joked to himself about buying a halo and some plastic cupid's arrows and becoming some sort of romance superhero. He'd get rich by using his unique abilities to help people see the rough spots in their relationships. So far it hadn't happened, probably because he'd never given it much effort. His talent so far had done nothing for him except paint most of his lady friends with appealing spots of green.

As he napped he smiled at himself, thinking about what they might call his little gift. *A unique ability. A special power. A superhuman insight.* He chuckled as he snoozed, hoping that anyone boarding the train would think he was crazy and sit somewhere else.

He yawned and opened his eyes to see a teenage couple sitting across from him. The young man wore gold chains around his lanky neck, and his Yankees cap backwards. Asleep beside him, a pretty girl with large hoop earrings held the young man's hand. Joe was quick to notice the conspicuous lime tint of one of her eyebrows. It could mean only one thing. Joe got up and sat next to the boy.

"Great start, kid," Joe said as he gave him a punch on the shoulder. "Atta boy. I've got eight myself."

"Huh?" the boy muttered, cringing and glancing at the other passengers.

"Oh, come on, I'm harmless." Joe waved it off and leaned closer to whisper, "Great start, you know, with the girlies, man..."

If both of her eyebrows had been green, Joe would have been quite impressed. But with just one eyebrow, the kid was obviously new at the game and could use a little encouragement. "So is your second girlfriend better than the first?"

Now the boy flinched and flicked his eyes at his companion.

"Kiddo, I'm *whispering to you on the 1-train*. She can't hear a thing I'm saying. No one can. See? Still sleeping like a baby." Joe grinned and gave a nudge with his elbow. "Never add one that you wouldn't trade for any of the steadies. If one of them finds out and leaves, it keeps you from regretting it."

The young man took a minute before blinking at the insight. Then he looked at his girlfriend for a moment, evaluating. His face lightened and he tried to hide a sly smile.

"Damn lucky work, kid," Joe laughed as the train slowed. "I like her earrings. You buy them for her?"

The kid shrugged no.

The train stopped, and as Joe moved to the exit he winked. "You should have."

Joe whistled as he strolled to his connecting train. He enjoyed letting his eyes dance across the hundreds of faces he passed in the crowd. He saw a few naughty green flashes among them, and he was pleased as he waited at the platform.

Joe saw green markings on those deceived in love.

It was simple, but he was the only person he knew who had that singular knack. It was a talent that had been with him for his entire life, though he remembered understanding it for the first time in fifth grade.

It happened when he was ten, during recess. It was the first time he had kissed a particular classmate, Denise, and the second time he had ever kissed a girl outside of family. They were hidden behind the trunk of a shade tree on the edge of the schoolyard, where he convinced her to let him secretly show her how to perform the wonderfully cute and moist smack of the lips. When he moved away to laugh and wipe away Denise's spit, he saw that half of her freckles had turned green.

When he told her, she didn't believe him. After he insisted that she go into the girl's room to see for herself in the mirror, she came back laughing, saying that she saw no change in her freckles, and that he was being silly. She even gave him a sunny peck on the cheek for making her laugh. All the while, in Joe's eyes, her freckles were as green as ever.

It wasn't until class resumed that Joe began to grasp the basics of this green phenomenon. As he left Denise to return to his desk, Joe noticed Hillary smiling from her seat nearby. Just the day before, beneath the same shade tree, Hillary had been the *first* girl outside of family that Joe had had the pleasure of kissing. His smile turned to surprise when he saw beneath her perky bangs a spot as green as the lawn outside.

Of course, both of them snapped back to their usual skin tones after Hillary found out about his kiss with Denise—or was it Denise that found out about Hillary? Joe grinned at the childhood memory and guessed that it didn't matter. He'd learned a lot of tricks since those days, and nowadays most of the women Joe knew unwittingly sported a spot or two of his favorite color.

With those fond memories in mind, Joe smiled all the way to Pub Donegal in the East Village. He *liked* the dim little bar because it was within crawling distance of his apartment, but he *loved* Pub Donegal because he had been infatuated with the evening bartender there for years. Diane was the most gorgeous woman he knew, and, of course, perhaps the only woman Joe considered entirely beyond his reach. Contrary to his own gift, she secretly possessed the uncanny ability to see cheaters in shades of orange.

"Diane, my unachievable objective," Joe called as he took a seat at the bar. "My match in battle, my nemesis. Tell me if you can see that I've been working on my complexion."

Diane greeted him from the warm darkness behind the bar and moved toward him, teasing him with slow and sultry motions. She slinked to the counter opposite Joe and splashed a greyhound in front of him, his usual mixture of vodka and grapefruit juice. As he took a sip, she studied his face. "Chiseled, handsome, features; stylishly old-fashioned trim to the hair; and a face as orange as ever. Punkin Head has just taken heartless advantage of one of his lucky seven?"

"Tonight, my secret seer of orange, I'm celebrating lucky number eight." To annoy her, he listed them in his customary ascending order, "Monique, Cassandra, Cindi, Beatrice, Sandy, Rochelle, Maria, and this afternoon Lizzy's ears, hands, and knees turned green before my adoring eyes. It means she's finally fallen for me."

Over the years, Joe and Diane had secretly shared between them all of the details of their gifts. On lovers cheated by their partners, Joe saw distinct green areas that grew larger, darker, and more numerous as the level of betrayal increased. Conversely, Diane saw the faces of those cheating become uniformly and increasingly orange as their affairs deepened.

"It's been a while since you've had your pitiful collection of wretches up to eight. Newfound Lizzy is the best of them?"

"You know it, babe. She's totally hot in her new green."

"Maybe soon poor Monique will be relieved of her green spots?"

"Maybe. Monique's had an excellent run." Joe shrugged. "You know, you'd look great in green yourself. You'd have a permanent place at the top of my list. Wanna give it a go?"

"For the billionth time, Punkin Head," Diane laughed as she wiped the counter with her towel, "I'd never date an orange-faced man, especially when it would turn my own face orange."

"And I'd never have faith in a greenless woman," Joe agreed. "How do you know that Boyfriend Billy won't show up orange from one of his business trips?"

"I just trust. That's what happens when you're in love, Joe. It's sad that you need to be told these things. Even though he's away in Boston, Bill would never put a green spot on me, see?"

Joe chuckled as Diane slowly danced and spun around. "I love it when you move like that. From the perfect curves beneath your t-shirt to your jeans filled to voluptuous perfection, I don't see even a trace of—"

"You don't see a trace of..." She came around to face him, and her smile faded. "Joe, what is it?"

"Uh." His fingers tried to gesture it away. "Nothing."

"Come on."

"Diane."

"If you're joking, I'll kill you." Her face twisted. "I'm green, aren't I? Tell me where."

"It's probably nothing, just a smudge from one of those drinks you're mixing." With a weak nod, he indicated a small space left of her navel, exposed between her jeans and t-shirt.

When she turned to give him a clear look, his mouth went dry. Despite what he had told her for all of these years, she didn't look great in green at all. His eyes betrayed that it was no cocktail smudge.

"You're sure?" Diane's eyes hardened even as they filled with moisture. When Joe nodded, the muscles of her jaw tightened. She folded her towel and set it down. "Then I'm going to Boston."

She swept up her things and disappeared through the door, leaving the bar to her puzzled coworkers. Alone, Joe sat and slowly finished his greyhound. He thought of Diane as he walked to his apartment.

The next day he stuffed himself, as he often did, with three lunches. With Cassandra he had slices of pizza on 33rd street, with Rochelle he munched on tapas in SoHo, and finally with Cindi he packed in a bowl full of wontons in Chinatown. He received hugs and kisses from each of his green-spotted darlings, and giggly promises of nights together as well, but all the while his thoughts returned to Diane's misfortune.

When he entered Pub Donegal that evening, Diane was back, her movements spiritless as she worked in the pub's gloom. When she saw Joe sit down, she tried to smile in greeting but failed. She mixed his greyhound and brought it to him as if it weighed a ton.

"You all right?"

"That bastard. I caught him orange-faced with another woman in Boston. He never came back orange because he'd break up with them at the end of every trip."

"Your green spot is gone."

"Good. And so is Bill. You promise that you never, ever saw a green spot on me until last night?"

"Promise." Joe made a sympathetic grin, but he wasn't entirely sure. He gawked longingly at her figure every time he visited, but because of Pub Donegal's darkness and the defense her special talent provided, he hadn't often checked her for green spots. He shrugged it off, smiled, and asked, "So now that you're available, are you ready to give it a go with Punkin Head yet?"

Finally she smiled a little. She made a rude gesture with one of her fingers and said, "Fat chance."

Joe sat at the bar and chatted with her. He kept the conversation light, not mentioning his three lunches or any of his eight green girlfriends. By the time he headed home, he was glad that Diane seemed to be feeling better.

He woke up the next morning and was pleased that only a slight headache reminded him of his evening at Pub Donegal. Hmmm, he thought, which of his sweethearts should he visit for lunch today? He wasn't sure he could pack in another three lunches so soon, but he was pretty sure he could handle two. He was brushing his teeth and trying to decide between Lizzy and Sandy when he glanced into the mirror and froze. He stared at his reflection, bewildered, as minty foam dribbled from his mouth. His ears, tongue, and neck were as green as any he had seen.

The green was still there after he spat out the toothpaste and rubbed his eyes. He tried an exfoliant scrub, but the telltale green remained. He had never seen himself like this.

What had he done to deserve such cruelty? Out of compassion and respect, he was extremely careful that none of his steadies knew about any of the others. Among all of their attractive characteristics, he chose them based on geography so that it was unlikely that he would unexpectedly and inadvertently cause an introduction between them. On top of that, he painstakingly prioritized and divided his attentions between them so they would never have reason to wander. Dumbfounded, he sat on his bed and wondered which of his lovely girlfriends could be so unappreciative.

It had to be Monique, he eventually decided. Just as he had advised the young man on the subway two days ago, Joe was diligent to add a girlfriend only when she was superior to any already in his collection. Though she was still nearly as lovely as any of the others, Monique had unknowingly achieved seniority within Joe's group, and was currently eighth on his list. Possibly with the recent addition of Lizzy to his assemblage of lovelies, Monique noticed that his affections seemed more thinly rationed, and her charms had been drawn elsewhere. Perhaps Pub Donegal's bartender had been right when she suggested that Monique might soon lose her green spots.

While he dressed, Joe phoned to invite Monique to lunch. Without any sign of deceit, she seemed happy to accept. In his experience, he had ended relationships with women eight fewer times than he had begun them. Today he was ready to reduce the difference to seven. He left his apartment with a determined energy.

At lunch, for possibly the last time, he admired the fragrance and island curliness of Monique's green hair. Eventually he brought himself to say, "I know you've found someone else, Monique."

Her dark eyes moistened and flashed at him. In the smooth Caribbean accent Joe suddenly realized he would sadly miss, she replied, "Joe, how can you say such a thing?"

"When I looked in the mirror this morning, I just knew."

"No, this isn't true. How can you accuse me?" She whined, her voice trembling. "I have been so good to you."

"Yes, you have," Joe agreed, putting his hand on hers. His heart rose to his throat. He had forgotten how difficult these things were. He preferred any emotion to sadness in a beautiful woman, and right now for Monique, he decided that anger would have to take its place. He told her about the seven others.

In a moment the green tint that pervaded every strand was gone from her hair. He had forgotten the jet-black beauty of her waves and curls, and to see it return he was happy for her. He was unprepared for the force of the slap from her right hand, and the furious splash of wine that stung his eyes. He writhed on the floor with the spilled silverware and toppled chairs while Monique made her feelings known to everyone in the restaurant, and to most of the people on the block and down Park Avenue, as well.

Holding the left side of his face, he got up and asked for the check. He waved to the stunned people around him and said, "That's all right, folks. She had it coming."

In the bathroom, Joe was disappointed to see that his eyes were bloodshot, a beautiful woman's handprint marked the side of his face, and his markings were at least as green as before. He cursed and staggered slowly across the city to the familiar gloom of Pub Donegal.

Joe sagged onto a barstool. Diane met him at the counter and slid him his drink. "I see that Punkin Head's had a rough day. I like the handprint."

"I woke up with green spots today," Joe explained between gulps. "On my ears and tongue and neck."

"You don't say." She giggled, but snuffed it out with a cough and a muttered, "Sorry."

Joe sagged a bit more.

"But really", Diane said. "With eight girlfriends, don't tell me you've never had green spots before."

"Never." He rubbed his sore eyes. "And for your information it's now seven girlfriends."

"That explains the beating and the smell of Chardonnay."

"And I've still got the green on me. It's getting worse."

Diane puckered her lips in exaggerated sympathy. "Well, just be glad that you're the only one who can see it. You'll always be good ol' Punkin Head to me."

"I can't go on like this," he moaned. He looked at his miserable, green-eared, green-tongued, green-necked reflection in the mirror behind the bar. Suddenly his face brightened. "Diane, I have an idea. You see cheaters in orange."

"Uh-huh," she acknowledged as she glanced around the room. "None of them are as Punkin-Headed as you, but I see two other orange-faced swindlers in here, about average for a Tuesday."

"I could take you to meet my seven remaining dollies

tomorrow. You could tell me which one's doing this to me."

"I won't." She didn't even pause to think about it.

"But Diane, why not? We have these gifts, and we can help each other. Just the other day I helped you—"

She put her hands on her hips and glared at him until he muttered, "Hey, I'm sorry."

She was silent for a minute before she spoke. "Keep dumping them until your spots clear up. Guaranteed cure. For you and for them." She wiped the counter in front of him and walked away.

Joe woke early the next morning. The left side of his face still stung from Monique's slap. He refused to look at the disgraceful, green reflection in the mirror. Instead he stuck out his tongue and crossed his eyes to confirm it. The green remained. Dismayed, he decided to try following Diane's advice.

If the green persisted, he would visit five of his remaining seven today: Beatrice, Cindi, Cassandra, Sandy, and Rochelle, in precisely that order. With any luck he wouldn't need to visit them all. He packed four clean shirts with him, just in case he needed them.

He met Beatrice for an espresso early. Fifteen minutes later, the green markings on her pretty neck, shoulders, and back were gone. Joe sorely realized how beautiful she was without them, but he had little time to be happy for her. When her brow creased with outrage, Joe presented the left side of his face to again be slapped. With caffeine-pumped rage, she slapped the *right* side of his face three times. *Of course*, Joe realized as his ears rang, *she's left-handed*. Before she stomped off to work and left him forever, she made sure his shirt absorbed what remained of her scorching coffee. Shirt one.

Half an hour later, after another cross-eyed glance at his tongue, Joe's feelings were mixed as he watched Cindi's green feet return to their dazzling natural bronze. Recalling that she was right-handed, he reluctantly prepared the tender left side of his face for the blow. Instead, she maced him from a pressurized key chain canister. He stumbled away in blind agony, and as a final goodbye, half of Number Six's supercooled smoothie hit him from behind. Shirt two.

Shirts three and four were called from the bench as

the day wore tragically on. He correctly predicted that left-handed Cassandra would slap the right side of his face, only it was enhanced by the remains of a California Roll that doused him with soy sauce and wasabi. Charming Sandy was the first of his ladies to draw blood with a closed-fisted blow, perfectly placed on his nose. Rochelle finished the day by splitting his lip and leaving his final shirt ruined as he stumbled into Pub Donegal.

"Great choice of attire," Diane commented as Joe slumped at the bar. "The blood stains match your eyes."

Joe grimaced as his drink stung his split lip. "I'm down to Maria and Lizzy and the green's still on me."

"Mad at me for not helping you?"

Joe shook his head after he gave it some thought. "You know, to see them snap back to their original color, it kind of made me feel good."

Diane noted his swollen nose, split lip, and the remains of coffee, soy sauce, pepper spray, smoothie, and blood that caked him. She said, "You look like you feel good."

Joe slowly nursed his drink, and then another, and after that, another. When he finally finished, he was numb enough to shuffle to his apartment without wincing. He rose and smiled weakly. "Thanks for not helping, Diane."

"Anytime, Punkin Head," she said. She watched him totter to the door, and in her magical vision his face was much less orange now. He looked good in the new shade. He had never looked better.

The next morning Joe awoke in the filthy trousers he'd worn the day before. He hadn't showered. A hangover filled his head to bursting. Unable to bring himself to look into the mirror, he stuck his tongue out at the ceiling and crossed his eyes to see it. He groaned when he saw that it was still green. Grimacing, he rose, squirmed into a tattered sweatshirt, and went out. He took a cab to Pier 84, where Maria, his second favorite of his remaining two girlfriends, spent her days operating tour boat cruises of the harbor. He anonymously boarded her boat and took a seat where she wouldn't see him.

As Maria's expert hands steered the boat from the pier, Joe tucked his own into his pockets and shivered against the chilly morning breeze. For a few minutes, he savored her voice as it poured smoothly from the speakers, explaining the various landmarks that passed to port and starboard. During the pause between the Statue of Liberty and the Brooklyn Bridge, he made his way to her booth.

"Joseph, what a surprise." She beamed, but her green eyes quickly widened. She touched his face with her green fingers, and Joe sighed with unhappiness. "But what happened to your lip? Your nose? Your hair?"

She had left her microphone on. Tourists overheard and turned to watch.

"Maria, darling." She was the third most beautiful woman he knew, and the second most beautiful woman he had ever kissed. He tasted her lips one last time, and it was wonderful as always, despite his injuries. He made himself go on, "The way I see it, there's one to two odds that you're cheating on me."

They didn't notice the gasps and giggles rise from the crowd of passengers.

Maria frowned, and her green eyes flickered to their natural blue, but back to green. "Joseph, what are you talking ab—"

"I'm talking about how I know that one of you is playing me." He winced and thought, that should've been smoother.

Astonished shouts came from the tourists as they began to gather around the booth.

"One of *who*?" The green flickered from her eyes and fingers once more. "And tell me what happened to your face."

"Uh..." Joe hesitated, noticing the gathering audience. He realized that he should've spent more time rehearsing this, but now it was far too late for finesse. Omitting any mention of magical green spots, he shrugged and told her truly how his lip, nose, and hair had reached their sad state.

Her suddenly blue eyes filled with furious tears. She shoved him and screamed, "Get out!"

He stumbled backwards out of her booth and nearly fell over the wall. The cold East River drifted past twenty feet below and behind him. The crowd of tourists cheered as

Maria leapt after him, pinned him against the rail, and struggled to throw him over. He held on for his life, shouting, "Maria, wait!"

A few helpful hands reached from the crowd, and Maria counted, "One...Two...Three!"

Joe tumbled overboard. The murky river gave him a brutal slap on the chest. As he choked on the frigid prop wash he saw Maria triumphant among the tourists, gesturing and jeering as her boat continued under the Brooklyn Bridge.

Joe stuck out his tongue and had a cross-eyed look. It was blurry from shivering, but the green was unchanged. It seemed the only part of him that hadn't turned blue from the cold. He groaned and started paddling toward the waterfront of Brooklyn Heights, and his voice bubbled in his wake, "Joe, your dumb idiot self just broke up with the wrong girl."

He heaved himself ashore and shook water from his clothes. When he emptied his shoes two small fish bounced back into the river. He scraped off a few handfuls of mud and squished directly to Lizzy's work.

Dogs yelped and banged inside their cages as Joe slopped up the stairs to her dog-training studio. He found Lizzy standing in the middle of her loft, holding the leashes of two of her student dogs. She was spectacular in her shorts and tank top, but Joe refused to let her gorgeousness distract him. Her ears, hands, and knees had already reverted back to their natural color. Joe saw that she had the nerve to smile.

"Maxwell, Sammy, sit," she commanded. The dogs complied, wagging their tails as Joe approached. She looked him over. "Joe, what happ—"

"Don't pretend to be concerned. You're cheating on me and I know it, Lizzy".

After a stunned pause, she said, "Joe, we've only been together for a week. How could I have time—"

Joe held up his hand and gestured at his ears, tongue, and neck. "I've got proof, right here. You can't see it, but I can. It's because of you that I've dumped Monique, Cassandra, Cindi, Beatrice, Sandy, Rochelle, and Maria."

She twisted the leashes in her hands. The dogs

raised their heads and perked their ears. Their tails stopped wagging. Lizzy muttered, "You're crazy. You come in here accusing me of cheating when you've been cheating yourself?"

Joe looked at his watch. Its motionless hands marked the exact time it was ruined by his swim in the East River. "Not since ten thirty-two this morning. You're the only one left, but now it's over."

Lizzy stared at him, her eyes tense and hurt. The sounds of the dogs in the cages echoed in the studio. Finally she took a shaky breath and spoke.

"Yeah, it's over. Goodbye, Joe." She dropped the leashes, folded her arms, and said, "Maxwell, Sammy, *kill*."

Leashes flailing like whips, two hundred fifty pounds of teeth and ferocious snarls sprang across the room. Joe turned and ran, his shoes slipping on the floor. Water splashed as he scrambled.

"Good doggie doggie," he screamed as he shoved the door aside. "Good doggie doggie."

He cartwheeled down the stairs. Pedestrians jumped for safety as he tumbled and sprawled onto the sidewalk outside. He clamored to his feet and dashed across the street, dodging honking cabs and buses. The dogs followed, leaping through the crowds. Trailing splatters of river water, Joe plummeted down a flight of subway station steps, panting and fumbling for his subway pass as he darted through the crowded corridors. People screamed and made way as the dogs charged after him.

He arrived at the revolving gate and swiped his pass through the slot. It blatted, denying him entrance. The dogs rounded the last corner and rushed toward him. He frantically rubbed the pass on his pants and tried again. This time the gate unlocked and Joe shoved himself through.

Sammy's jaws—maybe they were Maxwell's, Joe didn't know which—poked through the bars and ripped into the leg of his pants. The other dog reached through and grabbed the other leg. Joe heaved against the beasts until the seams gave way and the dogs pulled his trousers through the gate. In sprays of slobber, Sammy and Maxwell tore them to pieces.

36

Half-naked, winded, and girlfriendless for the first time in decades, Joe watched through the bars as the dogs made off with the remaining tatters. He was certain that Lizzy would reward the beasts with grade A5 Wagyu doggie treats when they presented their shredded prize. He took a deep breath and admitted that he and those dogs probably deserved their respective rewards.

Before the gawking crowd shifted its attention to Joe in his briefs, he ducked behind a trashcan and waited for the next train. He scurried into the emptiest car, curled up behind a seat, and tried to disappear.

"Hey, man, what's up?" someone called.

Joe looked across the aisle and groaned as he recognized the lanky teenage boy from the other day. Grinning at Joe, he wore the same gold chains and backwards Yankees cap. Beside him was the same pretty girl with the large hoop earrings and one green eyebrow. As before, she was sound asleep, leaning on her boyfriend's shoulder. But this time half the boy's nose was green, too.

"How are your eight babes doing, man?" the boy stage-whispered, flashing a conspiratorial smile.

Joe got up stiffly and forced a smile despite his scabs and bruises. "They're actually doing way better now, kid." He sat next to the boy. "And me, too. All I had to do was..."

He reached over and lightly patted the girl awake. She turned, frowned, and tensed a little when she saw the stranger in briefs sitting next to her boyfriend, both of them smiling.

"Hey, hot stuff, I've got some news for you," Joe said. "Actually, for both of you."

He gestured at the green areas invisible to all but him. The young couple exchanged a glance.

"You'd be a much better-looking couple if you'd stop cheating on each other."

The teenagers blinked, and then the boy returned the girl's glower. Joe rose as the train neared its next stop. He watched as their green spots flickered and faded, and their faces lightened and shadowed alternately as they made decisions. Before he stepped out, he patted both of them heavily on the back. "One way or another, I can see that you're doing better already."

Dashing between hiding places, Joe eventually arrived at home. He showered and shaved. He almost enjoyed the feeling of having a clear conscience for the first time since fifth grade. He smiled at the reflection of his normal-colored ears and neck in the mirror, and he almost bit off his tongue when he stuck it out and saw that it was still green.

"No!" he bawled, slapping both hands over his mouth. "It can't be."

It didn't make sense. He had wasted his entire collection of lovelies to rid himself of that defiling color. Had he abused his gift until it broke and failed him? Would he have a green tongue forever? He turned his back on the mirror as he dressed. He needed a drink. He made for Pub Donegal and slammed the door behind him.

He put his elbows on Diane's bar and buried his face in his hands. He muttered through his fingers, "There's something wrong with me, Diane."

"There's nothing new about that," she said, sliding him his drink.

"All of my girlies are gone. All of them."

"Yep. It's the first time I've ever seen you without that orange face." She smiled and came closer. "Hmmm, a very nice improvement. Guess I have to stop calling you Punkin Head."

"Maria threw me in the East River."

"And did you catch any fishies?"

"Two little ones. And then Lizzy's dogs stole my pants."

"That's a neat trick."

"You think you're funny, but my tongue's still green. What's wrong with me? I've lost my powers, or maybe I'm dying..."

"Lighten up, Joe." She laughed and rolled her eyes at him. "Or at least let me get you drunk."

"Go ahead and laugh it up. If I stay green like this, I'll never be able to trust a woman again. It's a hell of a price to pay for a clear conscience."

"You might have to learn to read the other signs like everybody else, Joe," she said. "You cleared up your ears and neck yourself, but the lingering green on your tongue *will* wear off. It says so on the label…"

From beneath the counter Diane withdrew a nearly empty vial of dark green liquid. She leaned curvaceously over the bar and handed it to him. Joe started to inspect the vial and its contents, but was distracted by the warmth radiating from her closeness.

She waved a finger at him. "Be careful with a bartender at her bar, Joe. It's a dye cocktail, totally non-toxic, I promise. I started spiking your greyhounds with it after you first mentioned your green marks. On the house, of course."

"Diane," Joe muttered. He frowned for a minute. "I guess I'll never know which one was cheating on me."

"Guess not."

"I can't believe you'd try to trick me."

"I didn't just try." She winked and grinned, squeezing even more lusciously across the bar. "So… Is that permanent place at the top of your list still available?"

Very slowly, his face made a hint of a smile. He looked into her eyes for a long moment. "You know, Diane, I think it just might be…"

In Days to Come
By Lisa Timpf

The poems in this collection are grouped into four sections. The first, "Terra, Terra," includes poems set on the planet Earth. That is true of many of the poems in the second section, "Looming Shadows," though they have been grouped together in relation to some of the potential disasters we as a human race have set ourselves up for—nuclear warfare, climate change, and so on. "Alien Encounters" contains poems relating to imagined interactions with other space-faring species. "Other Worlds" rounds out the collection with speculations on what life might be like if and when humanity spins out to the stars.

Type: SF/Fantasy Poetry
Cover Prices: Print: $10.00; ePub or PDF: $1.99

Ordering Links:
Print Edition:
https://www.hiraethsffh.com/product-page/in-days-to-come-by-lisa-timpf

ePub: https://www.hiraethsffh.com/product-page/in-days-to-come-by-lisa-timpf-2

PDF: https://www.hiraethsffh.com/product-page/in-days-to-come-by-lisa-timpf-1

The Oculist's Daughter
By Angel Favazza

The Oculist's Daughter by Angel Favazza is a steampunker in the old west. It's got a semi-mad scientist (her dad), her, of course, plus outlaws, Indians, Wyoming, a poison gas for killing natives, and an Indian guide. It all adds up to a rollicking adventure.

https://www.hiraethsffh.com/product-page/oculist-s-daughter-by-angel-favazza

The Muses of Summer
By Sandy DeLuca

Autumn's Come Undone
Sharmon Gazaway

Autumn stands before a large pumpkin. Her bare soles, planted on either side, draw up minerals from the rich loam. The pumpkin's skin, still warm from noon's heat, begins to glow, deepening from apricot to bittersweet orange. Stepping to the next pumpkin, she works the row, ripening each in turn, swipes her brow with her forearm, her hands grimy, and pulls the weight of her ginger hair off her hot neck. A murmuring rumples the tops of the trees, whispers forming words she can't quite make out. A chill lifts the fine hairs on her nape and she shivers.

Probably those air-headed dryads gossiping again.

As she walks to the brook to wash, honey-gold leaves drift down, cling to her hair like sprites. Humming, she pirouettes, her leaf skirts a swirl of marigold, russet, and spice. A garland of purplish-green globes dangling from the branch of a hickory tree catches her eye. She breaks off the vine and holds it up to the fading light.

Crow flutters to the lowest limb, his bent wing stiff.

"Muscadines," she calls to him. "Sol's favorite." She breathes on the globes and they take on a ruddier, sweeter hue. "Perfect."

She drapes the fruited vine across a low shrub on the brook's bank and kneels, scrubbing her hands in the icy water. The stream babbles at her, unintelligible at first. Dryads flit across the brook, tittering, cover malicious smiles with their hazy hands. She looks about, wondering where Sylvannah is and why she hasn't already herded them into their trees. She swishes the muscadine vine through the water, and shakes her head. It's a mystery to her how she ever endured the flighty things before Sylvannah came.

Crow lights on her shoulder, nudging her head. She shrugs him onto the bank. So little time left to prepare the table for Sol's visit tomorrow, and the muscadines will be the finishing touch. The brook murmurs insistently and Crow cocks his head toward it, turns and looks up at

44

Autumn. She leans down, listens carefully. The murmurs sharpen into words that glint and wound, and take her breath.

Rising, the soggy fruit slides from her slack fingers.

Autumn's leaf skirts rush and crackle as she stumbles through the darkening woods, throws herself beneath the arms of the Great Oak. She hooks her fingers in deep, harrows leaf-rot and worm castings, breaks her nails on the bones of birds and vermin. From low in her inner turnings a cry germinates, a cry that, breaking free, rattles branches and drives the dryads into their tree-skins.

She does not cry prettily. Not like Spring, who mastered the art of the one perfect dewdrop tear while they were still girls in Earth's nursery.

Moaning, Autumn rolls her head on the forest floor and grits her teeth, the moss clinging to her lips. She hears a crack inside her chest like the snap of a twig.

Pushing onto her hands and knees, she crawls closer to the Oak. She huddles between the roots, her back pressed against the furrowed trunk. She curls into her cloak, fastens the silver acorn brooch, and tucks in her bare feet, tight at Tortoise in his shell. Crow lights on her shoulder and roosts in her tangles. Autumn presses her wet cheek against moonshadowed bark, relieved Sol can't see her now.

All night she burns, shamed.

Like a fool, all day she hummed and danced while she worked, awaiting Sol's visit. In a large reed basket, she heaped the harvest's bounty—rosy apples, pomegranates, walnuts and pecans, lush persimmons. She set it on a table strewn with smilax vines by the brook. She savored the thought of Sol by her side for a whole day, wandering the meadow amongst violet and ochre wildflowers, drifting in a rowboat till moonset.

She presses her cold fingers against her blazing cheeks.

When morning comes, newly resurrected and only half alive, it sheds its mists and feeds on shafts of light. Light that colors everything the soft gold of Sol's hair. It fingers her face with tender warmth. She knows this touch —*his* touch—intimately.

Sol is mocking her.

She shudders to her feet, sends Crow flapping. She slaps twigs from her cloak, squares her shoulders and pulls up her hood, shielding herself from Sol's gloating.

This is not to be borne.

She marches to the brook, and heaves the table over. The loaded basket crashes to the ground, the fruit bruised and bleeding. She strikes her hands together and sparks shoot from her fingertips. The basket erupts in flame.

Shaking, rage unspent, she sets her face to the North and trudges out of her wood. Crow clings to her gray woolen shoulder, weight-shifting nervously. Mice dart and scurry for cover at her approach.

*   *   *

Whisking into vapor, Sylvannah slipped out through a knothole in the Great Oak when the wailing and gnashing of teeth began. All the other dryads shivered inside their trees. But she bit her lip and witnessed Autumn unravel.

Now, with Sol high in the eastern sky, and Autumn and Crow gone, the dryad's gossip chitters tree to tree.

"Sol jilted Autumn, even though she's never loved another."

"I heard he cheated on her with a star."

"No, two stars."

"They say he actually expects her to be happy for him."

Sylvannah listens, amused. Sol doesn't know Autumn the way she does if that's what he expects. She snorts. As if.

It was Autumn's silly sister, Spring, who else? A bigger flirt she never saw. Sylvannah began life in Spring's woodland where Spring was forever tempting this star and that to come down to her. And when they burned out on the way, her eyes, the yellow-green of a cat's, glittered. She clapped as they blazed and fell to cinders at her feet.

And now she's caught the biggest star of all.

Sylvannah shushes the dryads, and glides into the orchard. She simply can't see the attraction. Sol is larger than life, always seeking attention. Yes, yes his job is very important—but, nutshells, what a Golden Boy.

Autumn gave him her heart long ago. Sylvannah couldn't imagine a better match for Autumn. Fiery, everyone around her gets singed at some point. But Sol could handle it, even seemed to revel in her volatile nature.

True, Autumn is unpredictable, but she has a warm and generous spirit few in the wood ever see.

Sylvannah remembers the day many harvests ago when she discovered Autumn's forest. She watched from the cover of a pine thicket as Autumn tended to an injured bird.

"Stop skulking around the edges of the wood and introduce yourself," Autumn called to her that day, tying the bird's wing firmly with strips of linen.

Sylvannah glided out, one hand clinging to chunky bark.

Autumn glanced up and sighed, "Not another dryad." She ran her hand over the crow's ragged feathers. "So, what do you want?"

"I'm Sylvannah. I come from Spring's woodland. She —she banished me."

Autumn looked up sharply. "Why?"

"I suppose your sister didn't much like me telling her she was cruel, the way she taunted the stars to their destruction." She shrugged.

Autumn smiled tightly, nodded toward the Oak in the center of the wood. "You're welcome to live there. You're the first dryad I've met with some sense and grit. If you can keep those nosy airheads out of my hair, you have a home for life."

So Sylvannah did.

Autumn kept to herself, except for Crow, her constant companion since she saved him from a hunter's snare. On occasion she visited her favorite sister, Winter. But she sought out Sol more than any other, the way a wing seeks wind.

Sylvannah accepts this. All she needs is the shelter of the Great Oak, his rings of wisdom surrounding her, his constancy—home.

And bossing the other dryads is just gravy.

She weaves through the orchard, inhales the brewery scent of the apples that ache for Autumn's harvesting.

47

Among the shriveled, snaking vines pumpkins bulge to bursting. The trees breathe the colors of fire. As Sylvannah glides back toward the Oak, her lower lip sucked between her teeth, apprehension curls inside her like a little fog.

* * *

Autumn's sister, Winter, folds her into fur-robed arms and Autumn soaks up her warmth. Sol is weaker here. He and Winter always maintained a distant relationship.

"I know why you've come, Little Acorn," Winter murmurs into her hair. "But Summer will never agree to it." She frowns, her eyes black and liquid as a snowhare's.

Summer. The good sister who tries to bind them together. But she has a soft spot for Sol, friends since the Beginning. She will plead for them all to reconcile, be a family. Family! Accept Sol as a *brother?*

"Sister," Autumn snaps, flaring. "I didn't come to ask a favor. Or permission." She sees in Winter's eye the glint of indulgent pride her sister reserves for Autumn alone. It was Winter who comforted her when Mother left them like fledglings in an abandoned nest. Winter who endured her tantrums, taught her to dance like a dervish to burn off the fumes of resentment. "I came to give," she adds softly.

Winter takes her hands in hers and studies the black-rimmed broken nails. "Autumn, you're overwrought. With good reason. What Sol did—"

"What *they* did," Autumn grinds out.

"Yes. They. But with time—"

"Time? Time will only multiply the pain. The humiliation. There is no one else for me. Ever."

Winter drops her hands. "Still. I can't agree to this." Her pallid brow creases. "What of duty? Those who depend on you?" Her eyes harden like jet. "I will not take your silver acorn."

"When the time comes, you must." Autumn juts her chin. "I have no one else."

Sparks and ice splinters fly between them. Winter reasons, then pleads. Autumn will not be moved.

Winter, her lips trembling, swallows hard, and agrees.

* * *

With Winter's white realm far behind her, Autumn stalks through her own forest to the Great Oak, jaw hard. Snails—too slow to escape—crunch beneath her feet. Her skirts now blaze full-blown maize-gold, cayenne, bittersweet —mushrooms ride her hem like mum death-bells.

"Sylvannah," Autumn calls, gently strokes Crow's crooked wing.

Sylvannah floats down hesitantly from a branch high in the Oak, wavering before her.

"I'm giving my silver acorn to my sister. Winter will know what to do."

"What," Sylvannah rasps, suddenly still as lichen on bark, "have you done?"

Autumn kneads Crow's silky head, smears tears off her face. She takes a shuddering breath and shakes him off. He reels twice, then perches in the Oak, head cocked.

"You might want to glide to the highest branches," Autumn says softly to Sylvannah.

Eyes closed, Autumn imagines Spring, beribboned and blushing in Sol's light, melting into him—as she herself longs to do, still.

She begins to twirl, her feet an axis, her skirts whirring like a swarm of locusts. She spins, faster. Visceral heat surges up from her core, charges her fingertips, sparks fly. She hurls fingerling flames scattershot. One by one the trees ignite, sacrificed on the pyre of her rage. The gold and wine of a hundred sunsets combust. Oak, maple and pine pop and hiss their indignation—the screeching dryads flee.

Her skirts explode in a Pentecost of wildfire. And she twirls.

At last, the pain exceeds the one in her cracked heart.

*   *   *

Sylvannah drifts through the charred ruins, smoke permeating her gossamer heart. At least the other dryads are safe with their cousins in the river where she drove them. Crow crouches atop an armless black pine, head hidden under his bent wing.

She managed to save the Great Oak, whisking the flames away from his vulnerable upper branches. She caresses the gnarled, ancient bark. Below, something glints

49

in the ash. Swooping down, she retrieves the silver acorn clasp, icon of Autumn's power, for safekeeping.

And beneath it lies a smoldering, cracked acorn. Autumn's heart. This, she plants.

* * *

Winter comes to bury Autumn's ashes in mounds of pure white, as she promised.

Sylvannah fastens the silver acorn on Winter's furs, then glides up into the Oak's sturdiest branches and waits.

With Autumn's power, Winter is twice as strong. In time, Sol grows weak. Spring languishes, a pale shadow.

And Winter reigns. Some call it The Little Ice Age. Others call this particularly bitter time The Year Without a Summer.

Sylvannah calls it a reckoning.

"Autumn's Come Undone" first appeared in Metaphorosis in 2021

It Wasn't Silly Putty
Terrie Leigh Relf

Late last night, a cargo box was abandoned on the off-ramp to a local park. A packing statement found at the scene was labeled as children's toys, but none of the merchandise was located. Torn packaging of indeterminate origin was also located in trash bins at the nearby park, along with a pink gooey residue. Since no one has come forward to claim ownership, investigators are perplexed as to what occurred and who might be to blame.

taking imprints
of our children
alien archeologist

50

Carnival in Venice
Matias Travieso-Diaz

Won't you even give me this trivial thing,
so that after you leave,
it can accompany me in the loveless, pleasureless life
that is left to me?
E.T.A. Hoffmann, A New Year's Eve Adventure

In the fall of 1685, young nobleman Ernst Katcher fought a duel with a rival over the favors of a notorious French courtesan. Katcher was grievously wounded and it was uncertain for several months whether he would give up the ghost or stay with the living. At the end he recovered, but remained impaired: one of his wounds, a knife thrust to the leg, refused to heal properly, leaving him with a pronounced limp. Also, a vicious kick to the neck from his opponent now caused his speech to become blurred and sometimes unrecognizable.

Katcher was vain and considered whether to take his life, renounce the world by joining a religious order, or try to make the best of his impaired condition. He was still debating what to do when he was visited by his friend Friedrich, the scion of a noble house in Bavaria, who had been Katcher's second at the duel and had helped dispose of the corpse of Ernst's adversary. He found Ernst in a morose mood and tried to cheer him up.

"Look, Eri, you should count your blessings. Kleinmann died of the wounds you inflicted on him. You are still alive, are still handsome, and own a perfume factory that is guaranteed to keep you wealthy. Instead of agonizing over your wounds, you should spend the time enjoying yourself and leading the sweet life to which you are entitled."

"That's easy for you to say, Freddy, because you are not a cripple," blurted Katcher.

"You are rich and good looking. You are bound to be valued."

"Where? Here in Eisenach the noblemen are a bunch of stuffed shirts, and the women are as cold as the snows of the Zugspitze!"

"Maybe not here, Eri. You may need to travel south. Come, my friend, let me take you on a holiday to my favorite city. Let's get on the next carriage and go to Venice!"

"But Venice is a den of iniquity. It is the most corrupt city in the world!"

"Man, set aside your prejudices. You'll be appreciated in Venice as long as you bring plenty of money, because everything can be bought or sold there."

The trip to Venice proved arduous, for it was early February and the steep roads going towards Italy were covered by snow and ice. They arrived in Venice one late afternoon just a few days before Ash Wednesday. That was the time in which, by tradition, the last and best festivities of Venice's long carnival season were held. Their guest house, an ancient *palazzo*, sat right on the Canal Grande near the Rialto Bridge, an ideal location – according to Friedrich – from which to get involved in the action.

"First, we need to get in costume" explained Friedrich after they had left their bags at the guest house and gone out into the crowded streets. He guided Ernst to one of the stands where carnival supplies were sold. "In Carnival, we must disguise ourselves."

"What do you mean by disguise?"

"The good thing about the *Carnevale di Venezia* is that everyone wears masks and costumes, so nobody knows who you are and if you are rich or poor, even in some cases man or woman. You can do things that the rest of the year are considered inappropriate or illegal. You can drink, gamble, cavort with strangers, go whoring, pass out on the street. Nobody will think less of you, because everyone is out doing the same thing."

Friedrich selected a costume for his friend. "Here, Eri, you should wear a *baùta*." He picked up an outfit and handed it to Katcher. The bundle included a white mask, a *volto* that would cover its wearer's entire face, including the mouth, and would distort his voice. Also part of the costume was a tricornered hat and a large black cape that entirely hid a person's anatomy. "Now you'll be totally anonymous. Nobody will notice your limp or be startled by your speech."

"What will you be wearing?" replied Katcher, curious.

"I always like to dress like this: a *medico della peste*, a plague doctor. It has a mask with a very long beak that is used as a sanitary precaution by an actual doctor. The beak contains herbs that filter the air and cover the horrible stench of the victims of the plague, which is common in this city. I like it because it hides the foul smell of many of the carnival attendees. I will wear the mask with a long black coat, white gloves, and a staff to complete the costume."

They donned their costumes and masks and walked towards the Rialto bridge. The sun had not yet set, but they were already dodging figures with paper mâché masks adorned with fake jewels and feathers. There were children everywhere making trouble and emptying sacks of flour onto each other, as revelers walked in and out of drinking houses and private *palazzi.* On the canal, dozens of gondolas, flat-bottomed *sandolos*, and other vessels full of masked and costumed people sailed by, many of their occupants already drunk.

"What do we do now?" asked Katcher, bewildered.

"First, we find ourselves a café where we can get a meal and our first drinks. Then we start walking the streets. We will soon find impromptu parties on the streets and piazzas and more formal masked balls in private homes, to all of which we will invite ourselves. Bring a purse with coins to give away, but hide it well inside your cloak. This town is always full of pickpockets."

For the next few days, Ernst and Friedrich lived through an unbroken succession of masked balls, parades, regattas, and public and private parties. Their activities included vast amounts of drinking and dalliances with women of all ages and conditions. They were continuously amazed by the licentiousness of Venice's women, who sometimes would cast their costumes aside to display their bare breasts out of the windows of palazzi to entice visitors.

They pleasantly lost track of time until one afternoon, while the pair were having a very late breakfast of strong Venetian coffee at the Caffè Florian, Friedrich remarked with alarm: "today is *martedì grasso*, the last day of Carnevale. Tomorrow is Ash Wednesday and this town will close down."

"What do you mean?"

"You might as well be back in Eisenach. Venice in late February is cold and dreary. No more parties, no more easy women or even cross-dressing *gnagas*. Tonight will be our last chance to enjoy the wickedness of this city. Let's get going!"

"Truth be told, I am growing a little weary of all the partying, Freddy. Still, I'm good for one more wild night. *Vesti la baùta*, as someone would say."

***

Their progress through the streets and piazzas of the old city was slowed by encounters with partygoers they had met in previous days. By now, *I Tedeschi*, as the pair was commonly called, were a well-known sight among those enjoying the *Carnavale*.

They finally arrived, as night fell, to one of their favorite spots, the boat landing in front of the Ca d'Oro palazzo, a short distance north of the Rialto Bridge. There was a large street party in progress and they started their usual routine buying drinks for whoever they engaged in conversation. At some point, Friederich got entangled in an animated dialogue with a pretty brunette in maid's costume. Soon they disappeared into the shadows, leaving Ernst looking absently at the waters of the canal.

He was shaken out of his stupor by the arrival of an elegant *pupparin*, a fancy boat traditionally used as a *barca da casada* (family boat) by the wealthy families of the city. It was being propelled speedily by a pair of oarsmen, and carried two passengers sitting on wide benches at the stern of the vessel.

The woman was clearly quite wealthy. She was a strawberry blonde, with a mass of hair set in a complex pouf that utilized wire, cloth, gauze, and other materials to create a voluminous but exquisite coiffure. She was wearing an overflowing red gown and a jewel-encrusted velvet *moretta* mask that was held in place by a button in the mouth that prevented her from speaking. The bodice of the dress hung so low that her nipples showed, covered only by an opulent necklace of diamonds and pearls that protruded from her chest. She was wearing matching diamond and pearl earrings and a ring holding an almost black ruby the size of a quail's egg. In the light of a myriad candles set onboard, she sparkled like a living flame.

By contrast, sitting next to her was a man of indeterminate age dressed in a modest *arlecchino* costume. He wore a half-mask with a short nose and wide, arching eyebrows, and was dressed in rags full of multicolored patches. Though supposedly a servant in the *Commedia dell' Arte* tradition, he appeared more like a bodyguard or a pimp for the woman he accompanied.

The pupparin came to a stop right by the landing where Katcher stood. The woman lifted the mask so she could speak: her face was a fascinating mixture of innocence and malice, the delicate beauty of a Botticelli Venus and the hardened, calculating stare of a Carpaccio whore. In a rich alto voice, she greeted him: "*Buona sera, signor Katcher.*"

Surprise at the mention of his name shook Ernst to instant awareness. "Good evening, madame. How do you know my name?"

The woman issued a laugh that was melodious but devoid of warmth. "I make it my business to learn all that happens in *La Serenissima*. You and your companion have become well known during this Carnavale."

"What do you know about me?"

"Nothing bad. *I Tedeschi* have built a reputation for generosity and good humor that sits well with the memories set by other Germans who have come to our feast over the years. It is because of your fame that I have come seeking you."

"You honor me, my lady..."

"Please call me Giulietta. And I am no lady. I am a priestess of Venus, and it is my business to bestow enjoyment upon those who seek my services."

Ernst was taken aback by Giulietta's frankness. Recalling his near-death experience on account of his dealings with another prostitute, he responded carefully:

"Yours is a noble calling indeed. Yet, I have suffered on account of a previous dalliance with another lady of pleasure ..."

"Oh, yes, Gabrielle. She is very skilled."

"Do you know her?"

"*Mon cher*, we are a closely knit circle. I am in touch with every high-class courtesan from London to Warsaw. I rule Venice, as Gabrielle owns Paris. She told me about your eventful encounter with her last year."

"I see. Then you may understand my reluctance to jump into your arms."

"And yet I am prepared to make you a once in a lifetime proposal."

"That's another thing. The money I brought with me from Eisenach is almost exhausted. I am afraid I could not afford the favors of even the lowliest street walker."

Giulietta laughed again; this time her laughter was tinged with irony. "You could not afford my fee with all the money you own. But do not fear. I trade in intangibles."

"What do you mean intangibles?"

"Things whose value is not measured in coins. You *Tedeschi* are often willing to pay me with intangibles. For example, one of your countrymen, Peter Schlemihl, traded his shadow for the opportunity of spending one night in my arms. More recently, Erasmus Spikher gave up his reflection so that I would grant him one night of pleasure during Carnavale. Those goods have no monetary value yet they are appreciated by my master, who finds much use for them." She nodded towards her companion.

Katcher became a bit concerned. "*Signora*, I am a Christian. I believe the Lord has granted us mortal bodies that will one final day be resurrected and saved or damned for all eternity, in their entirety. I could not trade my shadow or my reflection or my immortal soul for a few hours of pleasure, no matter how sublime."

"My dear Katcher, what I am going to ask for is rather trivial, much less important than your shadow. It is something that leaves you with each use, but whose absence will hardly be noticed by others. I will spend this last night of Carnavale with you in exchange for your smile."

"My smile? How could that be of value to anyone else?"

The man in Harlequin costume spoke for the first time, in a wheedling tone that Katcher found annoying: "My dear sir, your smile is a manifestation of your joy. I have discovered a way to spread joy among the unhappy by injecting into their spirit the smiles of others more fortunate than them. For me, it is an act of charity that I perform gladly, for what is more generous than meting out the joy that this world needs?"

"Plus," added Giulietta, "there is no loss to you. You give one smile to me today and tomorrow you can give another to someone else, although your joy may be gone."

Ernst remained unconvinced. "This is either a fantasy or a lie. Why would you give me the pleasure of your company in exchange for a smile of joy? What is in it for you?"

"The details of my transaction with Doctor Dapertutto here are of no concern to you. Suffice it to say that in the deal I propose everyone ends up satisfied."

Ernst felt he had enough of this strange conversation and turned his back on the pupparin to go in search of Friedrich. Giulietta spoke again: "I'll give you a free sample."

"What do you mean?"

"Come aboard, sit with me, and I will give you a kiss that will make you want to accept my deal."

Fearing possible foul play, Ernst shook his head and started to leave. Giulietta, moving with surprising speed, got up and, assisted by Dapertutto and the oarsmen, descended onto the landing and stood by the astonished man. "Come, my dear, kiss me. What harm could there be in that?"

Ernst was more than half drunk and felt attracted to the mysterious woman. Turning to Giulietta, he asked dubiously: "Here in the street? In front of the Ca d'Oro?"

"Nobody is watching" she replied. "And we are only hours away from the start of Lent. Who is going to find fault?" Without more, she turned Ernst around, seized him by the waist, and reached up (he was over a full head taller than she) seeking his lips.

57

He obliged. Holding her by the shoulders, he bent his head and sought shelter in her luscious mouth.

For all he knew, their kiss may have lasted a few moments, or half a day, or an eternity. He lost himself in an ocean of pleasure, a joyous embrace that encompassed the whole universe and left him at the same time sated and desperately in need of more. When their mouths finally separated, he let out a long-contained breath and smiled broadly.

"See? You kissed me, you smiled, and you can do it again."

"So, what is the deal?"

"You sign your name to this paper, promising to give me your smile of joy in perpetuity in exchange for the services I will render, and then we retire to my room and you kiss me again, as many times as you wish, from now until dawn."

"Is that all? And I will wake up safe and sound in the morning?"

"What do you take me for? Do I look like a brigand? You will wake up after the best night of your life, though you probably will not have slept much."

"I still don't understand this deal, but I'm ready to have a good time. Lead the way."

Arm in arm, Giulietta guided Ernst Katcher into the night, Dapertutto following discreetly a few paces behind.

Ernst woke up with a start as the morning sun's rays bounced off the nearby lagoon waters. "I have to get up!" was his first thought. He was on the front steps of some palazzo, crouched against the front door. He rose painfully, trying to unlock his muscles. He was achy from the exertions of the previous night, but the fear of being arrested as a vagrant blotted out all other concerns, and he took off walking as fast as his stiff legs would carry him.

After a few minutes of aimless wandering, he came to realize where he was: the square known to the locals as Campo San Beneto, not far from his guest house. He made a couple of turns and reached the entrance to his home away from home as Friedrich was coming out, an anxious look on his face.

"Where have you been?" asked his friend as they almost ran into each other. "You were not in our room when I returned last night, and still were not there when I woke up!"

"I was … away" replied Ernst, not knowing how to respond.

"I hope you had a good time" smirked Friedrich.

For the first time since waking up, Ernst searched through his memories. He only had a vague recollection of doing something very pleasant that, however, left a bitter taste in his mind. Indeed, he felt gloomy and increasingly despondent. "I guess so," he muttered.

Friedreich's smile broadened. "It's fine if you won't tell me. We all have our little secrets."

Those words elicited in Ernst the realization that he, indeed, was carrying a secret, one that he dared not reveal even to his closest friend. He sighed and said nothing.

"Well, let's settle our house bill and take off before we get caught in the coming and going traffic" added Friedrich. "You will have plenty of time to let the cat out of the bag, if you wish, during our trip back home."

But Ernst, as he came to remember little by little his encounter with Giulietta, could not bring himself to part with his secret. He felt hopeless and dispirited, increasingly saddened at the realization that all happiness might have slipped away from him, never to return. As the day went on, he became at times snappish or morose, grunting or giving one word replies to Friedrich's attempts at making conversation and refusing to explain the reason for his moodiness. Friedrich eventually gave up and their trip proceeded in uncomfortable silence.

By the time they reached Eisenach, Friedrich no longer treated Ernst Katcher as a friend.

As time went by, many others deserted Ernst the way Friedrich had. Fellow noblemen, trades people, servants, the workers in his perfume factory, customers: all who came in personal contact with him were put off by Katcher's disagreeable personality, a state of affairs that he was unable to overcome. His business began to founder and he became increasingly isolated.

It was not as if he failed to notice the changes in his personality. To the contrary, he was aware that happiness had been stolen for him, and wondered whether he should look for Dapertutto or Giulietta and try to buy back his joy. Yet such a search might not yield good results; he now realized that they were demonic creatures of some sort and expected that the ransom they would demand for his smile would result in eternal damnation for his soul, a price he was unwilling to pay.

Early in December, Ernst decided he needed to make a quick trip to München to discuss with one of his suppliers the delays that were being experienced in the shipping of ingredients for his perfume making operations. After a day of contentious meetings, he left alone to have an early dinner at the Hofbrauhaus, a city landmark he had visited many times in the past.

He was sitting silently in a corner of the large tavern, nursing a tankard of the local beer and reflecting how his mood clashed with the joviality found in places such as this, when he felt a tap on his shoulder and heard a familiar voice:

"Ho, Eri, what are you doing here?"

Katcher's heart skipped a beat. Here was Friedrich, big as life, a man he had not seen in almost a year. How he missed his friend!

He felt guilt and a pang of pain. Trying to keep his emotions in check, he replied in as welcoming a voice as he could muster: "Oh, Freddy! Good to see you!"

Friedrich sat next to Ernst and ordered a beer. While waiting for the serving girl to bring the beverage, Friedrich stared hard at his once best friend, who had withdrawn into silence. "Say, Eri, we need to come clean with each other. What have I done to offend you? Why the long face when you see me?"

Ernst could not keep silent any longer. On the verge of tears, he replied: "No, Freddy, no. I'm not mad at you, there is nothing you have done. It is just that, since Venice, I have lost my spirit, and I'm always in a foul mood!"

The beginning of understanding lit Friedrich's face. "Did something happen in Venice? I had managed to get you in high spirits throughout our stay... except for the day when we got out of town..."

Ernst nodded, still silent.

"You were gone all night just before we left town. Did something bad happen to you then?"

Ernst did not respond.

"Come on, tell me. Did you commit a crime or did something awful? Did you lie with one of those filthy cross-dressing *gnagas*?"

At the end, Ernst could not keep his secret any longer, and in a halting voice told the story of his meeting with Giulietta and the bargain he had struck with the whore. Some parts of the story he could not recall clearly, but the bargain and the ineffable kiss that sealed it were as vivid as if they had occurred an hour before. "See, I'm damned" he concluded, disconsolate.

Friedrich then asked: "Are you sure you are no longer able to experience any joy?"

"I don't think so. I have been despondent since the last time we met, and nothing that I see or hear gets me in a better mood."

"We may be able to put that to the test. An Italian company is in town to perform during our carnival, the *Fasching*, and is doing shows every night at the opera house at Salvatorplatz. They do the types of comic routines we saw in Venice during the carnival. It is vulgar stuff only fit for the masses, but it should be good for a laugh or two. Do you want to come with me? If we hurry, we should be able to catch most of tonight's performance."

Ernst shrugged his shoulders. "Sure, I'll go, but I fear it will be a waste of time."

"We'll see" replied Friedrich, getting his coat on.

Although the theater at the Salvatorplatz was new, it was already becoming too small for the needs of the city. The place was packed with patrons, who laughed or shouted their approval of the slapstick performances going onstage. Ernst and Friedrich sat down and proceeded to watch in silence a series of short skits involving pratfalls, actors hitting each other with various objects, prattle in true and imagined languages. The audience hollered and guffawed.

Then, two actors went onstage wearing the garments of low-class servants ("Arlecchino" and "Pedrolino"). They started having an argument in barbaric German dashed with Italian and French-sounding nonsensical words. While the reasons for the dispute were unclear, the men were fully armed with wooden swords, knives, and pikes, and seemed ready to go at each other.

Their dispute was interrupted by the entrance of a burly man wearing the black cape and tight-fitting uniform of a Spanish soldier. He identified himself as "Il Capitano" and ordered the servants in a commanding voice to cease their argument. Arlecchino and Pedrolino did nothing of the sort, but continued to heap abuse on each other. Il Capitano sought to separate them, and then both servants turned on Il Capitano and pounded on him with their wooden swords.

The audience broke into raucous laughter, for the fierce-looking soldier cowered as a frightened girl and begged his tormentors to stop. At one point, however, Il Capitano wrestled one of the swords from the combatants and started pummeling Arlecchino vigorously, to the servant's loud outcries and protestations. Something strange happened then: Il Capitano's attacks became fiercer and his blows started drawing blood. Arlecchino's pleas for mercy rose in intensity as the comedian tried in vain to protect his face and limbs from the savage blows.

Other actors came onstage. Some tried to restrain Il Capitano, while others carried Arlecchino away. An astonished silence enveloped the hall, only to be broken by a single peal of laughter from the stands: Ernst had begun laughing uncontrollably.

Friedrich turned to his friend. "You are laughing!!" he declared in amazement.

Ernst was now laughing almost hysterically, releasing the pent-up emotions that had held him hostage for many months. He seemed to be going at it so forcefully that his entire body was convulsing, so Friedrich became a little concerned. "Enough, Eri, *basta*! Why are you screaming like this? What happened on the stage was only a *lasso*, a skit. And not a funny one at all!"

With some effort, Ernst Katcher calmed down. When speech returned to him, he explained: "I wasn't laughing at that stupid farce. That whore Giulietta mentioned how her other victims had given up their shadow or their reflection and could only get them back at the cost of their souls. I thought it was going to happen to me also, for losing all prospects of joy in my life seemed unbearable.

'But then I saw this actor, who in my mind stood for Dapertutto, being severely punished, and realized that, even if your joy has been taken away, you can still laugh. Other emotions can prompt laughter; for example, the satisfaction of taking revenge on your enemies."

"That may be true" replied Friedrich. "But it is unbecoming of a Christian, and a gentleman to boot, to take pleasure in avenging himself on his enemies."

Ernst offered no response to Friedrich's remonstration. He knew, in his heart, that his friend was right, but one avenue to recovery from the loss of his joy had been revealed, and he felt secretly satisfied.

Ernst went on laughing, even though the stage action was now an insipid romance.

It was the week before Christmas and Eisenach, usually a placid town, was ebullient with activity, as it celebrated the holiday season with its traditional Christmas Market in the city's main square and the courtyard of the Wartburg Castle. Ernst was in no mood for celebration, as was the case most of the time since his ill-fated holiday in Venice the previous year. Thus, he limped through the festivities, ignoring the array of traditional craft shops, strolling musicians, storytellers, vendors of baked goods and hot foods, and providers of mulled wine and brandy to ward against the cold.

For it was biting cold that week. Although warmly dressed and used to the cold, Ernst was shivering as he rushed to his offices near the center of town. When he reached the Marketplatz, which was relatively deserted because of the inclement weather, Ernst stopped to catch his breath and was intrigued by an unexpected sight.

Sitting on the frozen ground, leaning against one of the buildings that circled the square, was a tiny girl dressed in rags, holding a bucket in which passersby had dropped coins and items of food. The girl had a dark complexion and was foreign, gypsy perhaps, and was shivering from the cold and maybe from some ingrained hunger, for she was thin and privation showed in every muscle of her drawn face.

All the same, while shivering, the girl was tearing small pieces off a loaf of bread she held in one hand and tossing them at a few birds that had gathered around her. She was sharing her meager supper with other beings, just as unfortunate.

Ernst's first impulse was to move on, but the strange scene was compelling. He approached the girl and dropped a coin in her bucket. As he did, he caught a momentary glimpse of happiness in her face, and his own opened into a smile, realizing he had brought joy into someone else's life.

***

That night he sent a note to his friend Friedrich in München:

"Dear Freddy: Today I learned that a smile is not like a person's shadow, that can be removed once and for all. Instead, it is like the flowers in the field. There are of many types of flowers and many sources of laughter. Some may be gone altogether, but others will return next season unless prevented. I have been preventing all expressions of satisfaction from harboring in my soul. No more. I can still get pleasure from the world without enjoying what it has to offer, and can smile without rejoicing in another's sorrow. My life has been constrained by fate, but I can still live within my bounds and be content, if not happy."

The Wrong Princess
Kylie Wang

It was always a rude shock to be violently jolted awake, only to discover one's face to be buried in hay.

Once upon a time, the Second Princess of the Kingdom By The Sea pondered this fact as the wood beneath her jerked, again bashing the back of her head. Obviously, she was not in her bed, which was the last place she could recall being in. A rumbling around her ears told her that she was in a moving vehicle. A cart, perhaps. To her credit, it only took about half a minute to compute that she was being kidnapped, in her sleepy (and possibly drugged, judging by her sharp headache) state.

Strands of hay stuck out and poked her face in the pitch-black, like invisible hair. She strained against the coarse ropes binding her ankles and her wrists, trying to swallow the panic welling up like bile in her stomach, and thought about books where she might've read up on how to escape a kidnapping. But even though she spent her life reading more often than not (something her parents often grumbled about), none of the stories she knew were ever told from the princess's perspective. They always had a prince or a knight saving them.

It was quite convenient to be in a fairytale.

Maybe she should've read more "scholarly" books, like her older sister kept telling her to. Maybe one of *those* books contained a practical guide on how to undo a knot without the use of fingers.

Maybe she shouldn't have kept quiet about the several palace guards who regularly slept on their shifts. But that wouldn't be fair to her friends. They all worked second, some even third jobs in the day, and with mouths to feed, losing this stream of income could spell disaster. Still, being kidnapped was not a fun matter. She should have a polite conversation with Joe and the other guards about putting in a little more effort when she got back to the palace—if she ever got back.

No, her older sister would already be berating them. Although it was hard to tell what her reaction would be, since the First Princess always had a lot on her plate (and may not concern herself with the abduction of her younger sister). But if the busy newly-of-age did think enough of her younger sister to add "avoid future kidnappings" to her agenda, then the last thing the guards needed was someone else biting their heads off about their mistakes. Even though allowing a princess under watch to be carried off was *quite* the mistake, the First Princess could just be so... inconsiderate sometimes.

That was beside the point. Why the Second Princess was being kidnapped, she had no clue. Being the Second Princess out of three, everyone who had sniffed even half a fairytale knew that there were only three fates waiting for her: dying of a mysterious illness at the age of five, becoming a serpentine usurper of her older sister's crown, or being wiped off the portrait of history like a speck of dust. Obviously, she was the wrong princess to kidnap. If her kidnappers wanted a ransom, they would do much better with her older sister, the heir to the throne. Her parents would've paid any price for *her*. Even her younger sister would do—the fair, lovely Third Princess was doted on by the entire Kingdom By The Sea.

Not that she would rather her sisters be kidnapped instead of her, of course—but everyone knew that those were the facts.

The Second Princess moved her legs, trying to feel around to find the edges of the cart. Her slipper touched something—not quite solid, but not quite soft either. Were her sisters in the wagon with her? She felt silly for not thinking of this until now. No one ever kidnapped just the Second Princess in fairy tales if they wanted any sort of attention. "Hello?" She coughed, peering around in her haystack. Darkness wrapped tightly all around her, jostling silently with the motion of the cart. Maybe they had also been drugged and hadn't yet awakened.

A few minutes later, the wagon slowed down. She tried to wriggle out of the knots again, smoothing her breathing so she could listen to the jingling (of a padlock?) and creaking (of a gate?) outside. The Second Princess's whole body slid a few inches as the wagon jerked forward once more before stopping. The hay above her shifted. She felt most of it being lifted clean off her face.

There was a startled yelp, and an armful of hay fell back on her.

*   *   *

"*Silverware!* Our plan was to steal the *silverware!*" A voice hissed in the shadows.

"I am fully aware!" Another voice whispered back, more soft-spoken. "They just appeared in the wagon somehow! How was I supposed to know?"

The First Princess of the Kingdom By The Sea thought to herself that this was a horribly inconvenient time to be kidnapped. Winter swept nearer with each bite of sharp wind, and she had been working nonstop the past five weeks trying to stave off widespread starvation and war. In a couple of hours (for she judged they were approaching dawn), she was to be at a peace talk with the Royal Council of the Kingdom On The Mountains. It would've been a considerably better situation if she had been kidnapped the next week instead. But, as it was, fate often didn't schedule kidnappings at the most advantageous of times.

"Did you not check the wagon before you left?" The deeper voice again.

"No! I thought it'd look suspicious!"

"Oi! Untie me!" The Third Princess of the Kingdom By The Sea snarled at her captors, quite restless from being tied up for so long, as one feels after they've been tied up for a long time.

"No!" The two dark-shrouded voices snapped in unison.

"*Manners*," From the left of the First Princess, the admonishment spilled out of the Second Princess, an almost decade-old habit. From the sounds, the First Princess gauged that the Third Princess was on her right and the Second Princess on her left, both sitting against the wall like she was.

"We're very sorry for your situation, Your Highnesses," said the higher voice.

"What are we supposed to do now?"

A flame flared, basking the five people in a golden halo. First resigned to surveying her whereabouts, since it was hard to conjure up diplomatic phrases in her head while the argument fired all around her. Her two sisters sat on either side of her, similarly bound by their wrists and ankles. They seemed to be on the dirt floor of a... barn, of some sort. First wasn't sure, as she had never before been in a barn. (It was indeed a barn.) In front of her stood two young men who were really more boys than men, dressed in ragged tunics and trousers and deep in their heated conversation. Four grimy walls boxed in the wide space, empty except for a loitering horse, a wagon full of hay, and a few barrels against the opposite wall.

Third was still shouting for attention, because she felt nervous and that was how she dealt with it. In fact, without her arms crossed in front of her chest, making loud noises seemed like the only barrier between her and the world. "Untie me, and fight me with your own hands! Where is your honour? Where is your dignity?"

The Second Princess thought this quite improper for a princess, but remained quiet, because even the most well-mannered would not object to a chance at freedom. It would make a wonderful story, she thought, if Third really took them on and won. Books could be written about things like that.

"With all due respect, Your Highness, if we still had honour we wouldn't be stealing silverware for a living," one of them said, his crow-eyes deepening as he glanced at Third's sinewy forearms. He could probably beat her, the boy thought, but it was better to be safe than sorry. Besides, they didn't have time for that right then.

Even though Third was fit for a child who had just turned the age where children started denouncing everything they deemed childlike, she was secretly glad the scrawny boy-man had rejected her offer. He was a good two feet taller than her, and there were two of them, and, being a princess, she had never taken a beating before and wasn't keen to change that.

"Well then, let us go!" She huffed, swelling up her chest, because she deemed fear as childlike. "How did you even tie us up in the first place? You two seem awfully incompetent."

First felt her head throbbing as the sleep deprivation from the past few weeks weighed down on her eyelids. She was not looking forward to dealing with the letters that blanketed her desk back in the palace, which seemed to hop and clatter for her attention in the back of her mind.

"We didn't tie you up. We ended up with you three by accident." The nicer-sounding boy apologised.

"How do you *accidentally* kidnap someone?"

"There was probably another group of actual kidnappers," Second replied. "They must've mistaken your wagon for their escape vehicle." She had pieced this information together bit-by-bit, and was quite pleased for beating First to it, although, of course, she told herself it was hardly a point to be proud of. (First had, in fact, already figured out this fact, but hadn't felt the need to verbalise it).

"Anyway," said the other boy. "We can't let you go. You'd tell on us."

"But the guards will find us eventually!" retorted the nicer-sounding boy. "The whole city is after us. If we bring them back, and tell the truth, they might spare us." It was too bad that these two ended up with all three of the princesses, thought Second. If it had just been her, then no one would bat an eye if they ran off or came clean. The King and Queen certainly made that clear, thought Second, somewhat bitterly, recalling the way their eyes would glide over her, only to land on either First or Third.

"How do we know that?" The other boy was saying. "Better bring them along with us as hostages. We'll find Bridget, and flee the city—"

"What are your names?" First interrupted. It was against her upbringing to interrupt, but a fun fact about being kidnapped is that it would grate away anyone's patient and polite nature.

"We're not gonna—" The fiercer one said, as the other blurted "Jack" at the same time.

Not-Jack stamped on Jack's foot.

"Ow! Jesus, I'm *sorry*! It's a habit!"

69

First began to think that it might have been a bad idea to cut down the size of the royal guards in order to save up money for the city's food storage. If she hadn't, maybe she would've been in her bed sleeping, accruing energy for the long day ahead of her, instead of wherever 'here' was. "Listen, Jack," First said. "I need to get back to the palace. The kingdom is on the brink of war and I need to be at a meeting at noon in order to stop it. There's a huge amount of letters on my desk I'm supposed to answer, and there's this royal advisor who is definitely going to jump on the chance the second he realises I'm gone... it's complicated, okay? So if you could just let us go—"

"We're being kidnapped!" Third erupted. "Why are you still hung up on your *paperwork*?"

"Shut up, everyone!" Not-Jack grinded out.

First continued, "The point is, if you don't release us —"

"We'll make sure you and your families and your dogs all get hanged, that's what'll happen—"

"Now, let your sister speak," Second scolded Third, even though she agreed more with Third and didn't quite understand how her sister's politics would get them out of this. If anything, they should be trying to seduce instead. In the plot of a book she read, the princess that was kidnapped made the captor fall in love with her, and eventually convinced him to let her go.

"*The point is*, if you don't release us, we could end up with an invasion at the Northern Front, which isn't a matter to be—"

"*Everyone just shut up, or I slit her throat!*" Not-Jack yelled. In his hands was a short knife, glinting in the lamplight, pointing straight at the Second Princess. For the first time since the Third Princess woke up, all three princesses went quiet.

Not-Jack slumped on the ground. "Finally, I can *think*," he groaned. Jack sank onto the floor beside him. The Third Princess sneezed. So far, Jack was having the third worst day of his life—the first being the day his mother died, and the second being when the landlord demanded the debt his mother left behind be repaid by the next full moon. Now, they were faced with being kicked out of the basement he and Not-Jack (whose name was really Edward) and their sister Bridget lived in, even though Bridget was five and gravely ill and would not survive the harsh winter on the streets. But it was because the landlord's daughter was to be married in the spring, and her fiancé was a dirt-poor poet who couldn't pay for the wedding, and the landlord wasn't trying to be cruel, he was just trying to scrape together some money for his darling child's festivities.

That was two weeks ago, and the full moon was tomorrow. Not-Jack's job at the bakery only gave them enough money to eat, much less pay the rent. So Jack, being younger, more charming, and more innocent-looking, miraculously got himself a job as a kitchen boy at the royal palace. He spent some time gaining the cooks' trust, making friends with the stable boy and learning to ride, then snuck a satchel of fancy forks and spoons and sugar tongs into a wagon filled with hay.

But by the time he returned to the stable that evening, ready to flee, he took a wagon that had three live princesses instead. As a result, he and his brother were unlikely to survive the night. Because anyone with any experience with fairy tales knew that abducted princesses were always saved by a knight or a prince, who never failed to drive their swords into the hearts of the captors.

Right then, somewhere in the city, a group of wannabe kidnappers removed hay from a stolen wagon, identical to another one sitting in a dilapidated barn some distance away, only to find a sack of premium teacups instead of the tied-up cargo they were expecting

"We can still return them," Jack implored. "Say it was an accident."

"We promise not to tell anyone who you are," The Second Princess offered, eyeing the knife Not-Jack had placed on the ground.

"No," Not-Jack murmured, his calloused fingers wrapping back around its hilt. When he looked back up, there was a cold gleam in his eye to match the blade. "We have to run. It's the only way we can make it out of this alive. Me and you and Bridget." (Despite the shivers crawling down her spine, Second imagined Bridget to be

71

spelled with two t's because she thought it looked more romantic). "These three are dead weight. They won't be able to snitch if they're not alive to say anything."

"No! We're *not* killing people!" Jack exclaimed.

From far away, a horn was blown, the sound seeping through the thatched roof of the barn.

"In any case, it's too late," said the First Princess.

* * *

Not-Jack jumped up. "What was that?" He pointed the shiny knife at First.

"They're locking down the city," She replied calmly. "If you were thinking of escaping, you've lost your chance. Soldiers are going to fill the streets in just a moment."

He groaned. "How did this all go wrong?" He muttered to himself. "It was just a simple plan to steal some silverware for money, but *somehow*—"

"Your plan wouldn't have worked anyway," said the Second Princess. All eyes turned to her, and she pinked. "Jack worked as a kitchen boy, right? Kitchen boys come and go, and I hear stories from the cooks about them making off with silverware every week. It's why they don't put the valuable ones anywhere they can access. It's locked up in one of the rooms higher up, and they bring them out for meals..."

Not-Jack pinched the bridge of his nose, and First's shoulders lowered at the sight of a motion she was so used to doing (in private, of course, for the First Princess was taught to never lose her composure in front of others). "Jack? A word."

The duo made their way to the corner of the barn with the wagon and the horse.

The First Princess sighed. "You okay?" She nudged Third, who rolled her eyes because that was cooler than being afraid and muttered, "Why wouldn't I be?"

Even though there were several obvious answers to that question, First let her sister keep her façade, and turned to Second instead. "What about you?"

"Oh, I'm fine. I'm sure your diplomatic skills will get us out safely." Second said in a tone she considered neutral. She was, in fact, quite dubious of her sister's so-called 'diplomatic skills.' She used to pride herself in being the most sociable of the three siblings, but ever since First started tagging along with their parents at long gatherings with important people, the adjective was unanimously switched over to her.

First had dealt with enough people to notice the not-so-subtle sour hint in Second's tone, regardless of whether or not she had respectable diplomatic skills. "What?"

"What? I didn't say anything." (Second may have many things she wanted to say to First, but didn't want to engage in an argument, preferring to vent her frustrations behind her sister's back.)

"*What* are you upset about?" First was used to Second taking her side when they were disagreeing with Third, or else staying out of the way when she had things to do. She took a deep breath and told herself that anger was not a regal emotion, and frustration was just a branch of anger.

"Nothing, nothing much. I just... I just wonder if there's a more effective way than begging them to let you do your chores."

First closed her eyes and took another deep breath, telling herself not to question her absentminded sister's knowledge of hostage negotiation. "For example?"

"Well, we could try to escape, for one," she said.

"I *have* been trying to escape." First raised her bound arms. She was, after all, the Future Queen of the Kingdom By The Sea. She was brought up to always think of everything, even when her attention swirled obsessively around letters and duties and meetings. "We won't be able to get off the floor before they kick us over."

"Even from here?" Second challenged. "They're quite far away, and they're not paying attention." In her mind, she was imagining an epic fight scene, where she shoved Not-Jack onto the ground in order to save First. (After which she would turn to Jack, who would put up his hands and shake his head, his dark eyes glittering most romantically.)

"Not-Jack is." Being the Future Queen, she was also brought up to notice everything, and she had been noticing his glances over at the three princesses for some time.

Beside her, the Third Princess snored. Only she could fall asleep in a place like this, thought Second.

"I just feel as though... the way you're going on about your papers... they could easily only let you go, and keep us two."

"That's fine," said First. Second bristled. "I'll just lead all the guards over here," First continued. "They'll save you two."

"Is that what you were thinking about, though?"

Being of her intellect, First had formulated this plan earlier, of course. But she kept quiet, since getting her sisters out of this situation hadn't been on the forefront of her mind until now.

Normally, Second was not a confrontational person. In fact, disagreeing with people made her nervous. She often resorted to conveying her dissent through exaggerated agreeableness and elongated silences. *An invisible bite*, her ladies-in-waiting would joke. But something about First's wordlessness stirred up a well of complaints, pent-up from much longer than just that night alone.

"I mean, are you even worried about our safety? It's almost like you forget we're being *kidnapped*!"

"Oh, we're not in danger," First dismissed. The further along the night progressed, the less respect she had for their two 'captors.'

"How can you be sure? We don't know them! We don't know what they can do!" Second couldn't as easily forget the image of the silver blade at her throat. "If it weren't for the city alarm, they would've killed us so that they could get away!"

"Jack would've stopped him." First injected a confidence in her voice she didn't quite feel. In every other situation, she would've been *fairly* certain from the look in his eyes, the way his brow furrowed and his lips trembled. But it just happened to be so that murder was not a very lighthearted subject.

"How would you know?" Second somewhat believed First, in fact, but now that she was gaining the upper hand in the conversation she wasn't ready to let it go. Years of holding one's breath, of standing by and smiling graciously while one's sister received showers of praise and rewards, often did that to someone. Besides, it wasn't fair for First to be gambling all three of their lives.

First didn't have a tangible reason for her belief, so she elected not to speak, the grooves between eyebrows carving deeper and deeper. She hoped for Second's sake as much as her own that her sister would just let go of this subject.

But Second wasn't the careful diplomat that First was used to dealing with. "Even if we were actually kidnapped by actually competent kidnappers," Second snapped, "You would still be more worried about the state of the kingdom, wouldn't you? You wouldn't care whether we lived or died, *would you?*"

The last question was uttered so loudly that both Jack and Not-Jack turned to stare from twenty feet away. Second dropped her gaze. As soon as the words left her mouth she wished she could snatch it back, as one does after they yell something particularly mean at their sibling.

First's breathing came in short puffs, as she curled and uncurled her fists. Anger is not a regal emotion, so she closed her eyes and chanted to herself in her head. Her teeth pressed together so much it hurt. Anger is not a regal emotion. It is neither productive nor dignified nor benevolent.

If this were to become a shouting match, First could win without trying. But the worst part was that Second was right—a sensation First was quite unused to, being the Future Queen of the Kingdom By The Sea. Because anyone who had ever sniffed even half a fairytale knew that being the First Princess was the wrong princess to be, despite the praise and the adoration and the aptitude at everything she touched. Because when you were the First Princess, you weren't really a princess at all, you were only the Heir to the Throne. And when you were the Future Queen, you had to be a servant to your people, however tiring or limiting or taxing your duties were, because every day there were thousands of five-year-olds with wide doe eyes and mysterious illnesses who counted on you to get them through the harsh winter.

And when a hundred thousand people demanded your unwavering attention every hour of every day of every year ever since you were twelve, it piled on you and crowded out your ability to feel or think about anything else. Because when you were the Heir to the Throne, and you woke up to discover that you were kidnapped in the middle of the night, your first and only thought was what would happen to the kingdom if you disappeared for a day, or a week, or forever.

But how would you explain that to a girl who giggled while sharing secrets to the palace maids she befriended? How would you explain that to a girl who'd just had her first taste of young love, a girl who would try to calculate the fluctuations of the Royal Treasury but end up doodling fantastically-shaped trees in the margins? How would you explain that to a princess who was not an heir? How would you explain that to a sister?

First looked away instead of trying.

"Can you two quit it, please?" The Third Princess spoke up. The other two had almost forgotten that she was there, as one often did when the person in question was pretending to be asleep to avoid participating in a tense conversation between her two sisters, both of whom she secretly looked up to, although she would rather down a bucket of hay than admit it. Her voice was smaller than her usual (raucous, Second would say) volume. "I want to go home."

The three princesses fell silent.

Not-Jack returned from their corner at that point, with Jack shuffling, head bowed, in tow. Grateful for the change of focus (and the excuse not to apologise), Second turned to look at them. "Well?" She asked.

"We figured it out," Not-Jack declared. "The city is under lockdown by now, right? There's very little chance that we can escape. So we're going all in. We're announcing that we're holding you three hostage, and we're demanding ransom and safe passage out of the city, along with our sister."

"That is a horrible decision," Third said.

"You two are awful at this," Second seconded. Despite herself, she started worrying for them. It had been quite some time since they were discovered missing, and she knew that any moment now a knight (for a handsome young man in shining armour was sure to come rescue them) would appear, and how would Jack and Not-Jack then explain that the current circumstances were entirely by misfortune?

Almost without thinking, First knew their plan would never work—in order to avoid arrest, they would have to clear out of the entire kingdom, since holding none other than the Future Queen of the Kingdom By The Sea hostage would entail no less than death for their entire family. No nearby kingdom would be willing to let in a pair of scrappy boys through their borders at a time like this, with war brewing like a storm on the horizon. This was assuming that their trick of holding the princesses hostage would work in the first place, since a team of the best in the kingdom would be onto them to rescue the princesses the very moment they revealed their location. And this was saying nothing of how Jack and Not-Jack would be able to get hold of their sister, since she would immediately be taken in order to negotiate a trade.

"We're very sorry," Jack added, fidgeting with the edge of his tunic. Second bit her lip, trying to figure out how best to comfort him. "And we're not demanding much. Just two hundred and fifty shillings. Just enough to pay off the debt, and buy medicine for our sister, and find new jobs and start a new life somewhere else... Our sister Bridget is very sick, you see, she's only five, and if we get kicked onto the streets she won't be able to make it through the winter, so we really have to do this, you see."

"I'm not here to listen to your tragic sob story," Third grumbled. Even she didn't know what she was angry about, though. All she knew was that, slowly but steadily, she had taken a liking to the two boys-turned-men.

"Hey, hey, we can still fix this," Second said.

"Help them," Third pleaded, nudging First. "Come on, think of something. Aren't you supposed to be the smartest one here?"

There was a second's pause as Second decided whether or not she and First were on speaking terms. "Yeah, help them," Second agreed reluctantly, avoiding eye contact.

First closed her eyes, taking deep breaths and trying to shove away any thoughts about kingdoms and meetings and wars. She continued taking deep breaths until she had wiped away all the parchment letters and ink-scrawled numbers and sleek, oiled beards of royal council members printed into the back of her eyeballs. After a long while, only the back of her eyelids remained, burned red from the lamp fire in front of them.

Then she opened her eyes, feeling a warm energy surge into the empty space. Because despite her various faults, the Future Queen was really, *really* good at one thing—helping people.

*   *   *

A pair of royal guards found the three princesses banging on the door of a barn door, asking to be let in. They were shocked that no one saw where they had emerged from, since the streets were swarming with armoured soldiers and palace guards patrolling and knocking at front doors. And they raised a brow as to why the princesses chose to knock on a random barn, but obviously the princesses were in shock, so who would blame them? Besides, they listened with growing alarm to how the First Princess described the empty streets for several blocks, without a single guard in sight, her voice rising at the lacking diligence of all those on patrol—so since she willingly changed the subject, who were they to bring this up to their superiors?

And when they and a number of other guards broke into the barn, all they saw were a grimy horse, a wagon of barrels in the corner, and two scrawny, completely harmless-looking boys fast asleep on a stack of hay. The princesses said that their captor had left them alone and made off, allowing them to escape and seek help.

No one noticed the small hole in the wall, edges too sharp to have been bitten out by mice—in fact, looking a lot more like it had been carved with a knife—just big enough to peek through at the street. Nor did anyone notice that the horse seemed stronger and better-fed than what a normal peasant would own. It was dark that night, after all.

Before climbing into the carriage called for them, the First and Second princesses glanced at each other. They held their gazes, and a mutual understanding (forgiveness, maybe) seemed to pass silently between them, the way it only could between siblings.

*   *   *

While cleaning the Second Princess's quarters the next day, one of the ladies-in-waiting did notice that a necklace—one that the Second Princess held dear and slept with every night—had disappeared. That particular lady-in-waiting was very close to the Second Princess, and she happened to have a matching necklace, a gift from the Princess herself. But with a big smile, the Second Princess said not to worry, she would buy them both another one. It wasn't very expensive to replace anyway—only about two hundred and fifty shillings.

The kidnapper was never found. Firstly, the Future Queen herself had insisted the city gates be open the very next day, and of course he must have escaped as soon as that happened. Secondly, the princesses themselves never agreed on a description of the kidnapper—the First said he was tall and thin with a sweeping black cloak, the Third maintained that he was a large, redheaded man, and the Second kept telling them both that the kidnapper might have been a woman, and they shouldn't make assumptions about what a woman could or couldn't do. And thirdly, all three princesses were alive, unharmed, and wholly unbothered by the encounter—so who would blame the royal guards for slacking a little in their search?

*   *   *

At dawn when the three princesses returned, the King was waiting anxiously in the courtyard. When the princesses stepped out of the carriage, he embraced the First Princess first, because she was after all the First Princess, and her state of being alive was invaluable in running the kingdom. Then he held his arms out for the Third Princess, who for a second held back, scowling at all the eyes on her—before she changed her mind and sank into her father's hold, hugging him back.

The Second Princess awaited her turn, and afterwards left the Third describing the vivid emotions of the night (but skimping over the little details). First was already nowhere to be seen.

Holding back a sigh, Second trekked alone back to her quarters.

When she opened the door, she was met with a sea of wide eyes. She blinked, and a thunderous cheer rang up.

Delighted faces welcomed her in, because although she was not the First Princess, the Second Princess's state of being alive was still invaluable—maybe not in running the kingdom, but she was still invaluable nevertheless.

Some hours into the party, Second slipped away, and knocked on the door of the study. Like she expected, her older sister sat with her back wood-straight at her desk, with papers sprawled all over the massive surface.

"Come on, there's a party you should join."

"I have a lot to do," The Future Queen grumbled. "And I have a meeting I need to attend at noon."

"They're happy to see you back. Plus," she looked around and leaned forward conspiratorially. "There's cake."

It took another ten minutes before Second convinced First to take her first break in five weeks. Because contrary to First's unpopular belief, being kidnapped was a perfectly reasonable reason to be unavailable for diplomatic talks, and so was recovering from the event for a few days, even a few weeks if she wanted. But, of course, being the First Princess, she only allowed herself a three-day vacation. It was still the sweetest three days of the past couple of years. She was relieved when the kingdom did not erupt in flames during this time period.

*   *   *

Many years later, somewhere in the city, a man named Jack, his brother Edward (who was not named Jack), and their sister Bridget bought a barn that they remodelled into an inn. They made enough money to fill it up with expert-made sugar tongs, delicate teacups, and silver spoons—as well as scrawny boys who tried to steal them.

*   *   *

To say that the three princesses—eventually two princesses and one queen—lived happily ever after would be incorrect. They didn't always live happily, and they certainly didn't live ever after. But they each lived a good long time, and the Kingdom By The Sea prospered for the majority of it (after all, its ruler was really, *really* good at helping people, which in the end was all that mattered). Some more ill five-year-olds may have been buried in the winters, for grief was a constant fact of life, but every year there were fewer than the year before. The Second Princess held the palace intact while her older sister worried about the kingdom, making friends with all the guards and cooks and kitchen boys throughout her lifetime, although her sisters always remained her closest companions. Once in a while the First Princess, who became the Queen, would fall sick of mysterious and undetectable causes and be unable to complete her duties, only to be cured by a sunny picnic in the palace garden. The Second Princess and the Third Princess would join her on her annual sick leave, and they would all talk and laugh and sip tea in the warm summer breeze.

And that was all they could've wanted for each other.

Untitled Tanka
Tyree Campbell

fall of Earth
controlled numbers
human mating season
alien reproduction permit
rose-scented sheets

published in May 2005 Scifaikuest

Winds Of Change
Cameron Cooper

On the third day after the Winterwillow Collective changed routes, they reached what should have been the Aberuthen Warren. The valley which greeted them was not as it should be, which didn't reassure Saima.

She trusted Pallas. Of course she did. He was her husband. Only he had looked so *strained* lately, bent over his books and data. And he had argued so strongly with Director Brid, until it seemed that Pallas had forced the Director to declare the Collective would visit Aberuthen, instead of Director Brid coming to his own decision. Then Pallas had insisted upon walking behind Brid as the Collective travelled north-west.

Saima and Markas, her other husband, had walked with Pallas at the head of the file. They could scarcely do anything else. They'd given their wagon to one of the relief drivers.

Now the slow-moving caravan of creaking salvage carts, enclosed living wagons and mongrel vehicles came to a halt behind Director Venkat Brid as he pushed back his hood, unhooked his face veil and stared out across the shallow valley they'd reached. Everyone gathered behind him and spread out across the low crest to study their destination.

Saima pulled aside her own veil and sniffed the air. It was close to dawn and the omnipresent ivory dust was minimal. She lowered the veil, but left her hood in place.

Under the thick, permanent cloud cover, there was no moonlight to illuminate the valley. Saima only knew what moonlight was because she had grown up on a platform. Yet the bone-white, bare, heat-baked and sterile earth told its own story, for it lay across the valley like a winding sheet, pale in the night and bereft of details.

"Where is the Warren?" Director Brid demanded. "The lobby should be right there."

Saima rested her hand against Pallas' back as he tensed. She soothed silently.

"What did their lobby look like, Director?" Markas asked. He spoke with the smooth, placating tones he used when examining witnesses and pronouncing judgements.

"It's been twenty years. More!" Brid sounded disgusted. "I can't remember. It was wider than it was tall. Corrugated steel and girders. Sturdy. It's not there, now." He held out his hand. An assistants thrust the battered, scratch and cherished binoculars into it.

Brid studied the valley in detail. "This is damned peculiar." He lowered the glasses. "The entrance is there, but nothing protects it." He brooded, weighing the safety and wellbeing of the Collective. He turned, his boot heel under the djellaba digging a round hole in the white dirt. "Pallas, did you know something had happened to the warren?"

Saima stroked Pallas' spine, where the Director couldn't see it, reminding Pallas that his skills were valuable, that he must trust himself and remain firm.

Pallas shook his head. "The data doesn't give details, Director. The patterns merely suggested we should head in this direction."

Pallas was an unregistered asset. He served formally as Markas' secretary and archivist, for Markas was the registered asset in the Collective. But Pallas' real talent was an ability to absorb and process huge amounts of data. He could see patterns in datasets, and across them, too. Unlike assets who could also memorize vast seas of information and spot trends, Pallas specialized in social and anthropological movements. He was very good at what he did, even though it often meant he was preoccupied with feeding his mind with data, a furrow between his fine brows. He consumed information, his narrow chin down by his chest, working to retain it. Sometimes Saima found it hard to draw him back to the real world, to share a meal with her and Markas.

"We'll go down there," Venkat Brid decided. "Find out what happened and lend a hand if they need it. Collectors, spread out. Let's do a sweep across the valley. We might yet profit from this detour."

He handed the glasses back, replaced his veil and dug his hiking pole into the ground. The Collective shifted into slow forward motion.

Saima swayed so she could see Pallas' face. He was a very tall man for a Collective-born, which meant their eyes were level. Over the top of his veil, his looked silver in the last of the dry, dark night. He picked up her hand. "I'm fine," he assured her. He tugged her into following Venkat Brid down the hill toward the remains of the warren they had come to trade with.

*   *   *

As they approached the entrance to the Aberuthen Warren—a wide set of rammed earth steps heading down to the forum level—more signs of trouble reached them.

The outrunners reported back that a motherlode of salvage was in the valley, but scattered like sand particles, not grouped in huddled remains of what once had been buildings.

Also, the warren steps were not shielded from the elements. Old girders thrust from the ground, bent and twisted, showing mangled, unweathered steel between rust. They marked in metallic Morse the shape of the building that had once protected the entrance.

The wall that staved people away from the rear of the stairwell pit remained. It was made of old, massive Hedonist concrete chunks bound together with rammed earth and slathered over with straw mud.

"No lobby, salvage lying across a valley that was picked clean a generation ago..." Brid muttered. He looked up at the sky. "Dawn, soon. We can't linger here to figure this out. Pallas, you said it would be worth while heading here. Go down there and see if the weather seal is in place. Rouse them, if it is."

Pallas pushed his hood back and unhooked his veil. Markas handed Pallas their solar torch. Pallas switched it on, then trod down the steps, the bright, focused beam playing ahead of him, before he and the light disappeared beneath the earth.

Another scout ran up. "Their power dish is misaligned, Director."

Saima pressed her lips together. Power collectors were built to endure. What force had wrenched it out of alignment?

84

"Fixable?" the Director asked. "Within the engineers' skills?"

"They say yes."

Brid nodded, as the solar torch lit the upper steps of the warren entrance once more. This time, many people emerged, climbing behind Pallas, all of them in the loose, many-layered clothing of the warrens.

One of the taller among them lifted her arms. "Venkat Brid! I see and breathe!" She encased Brid in a hug determined to compress him into a sliver.

"Grazia Ederne," Brid said breathlessly. "You're leading Aberuthen?"

The stout woman stepped back. "Two years, now. I cannot believe Winterwillow is here at my door." In the light of the solar torches springing up around them, her face looked worn, her eyes drawn by lack of sleep. "We are in dire need, Brid. Does your Collective still have a Judge Jurist among its assets?"

Brid nodded. "We do. You are in need of one?" He looked around the remains of the building that had once protected the warren entrance. "I'd have thought you'd be in need of engineers. Your dish is misaligned."

"Those, too," Ederne said, gripping Brid by the elbow. "But we are more sorely in need of a judge. We have trouble. Criminal trouble. Come. All of you. The warren is still awake. Let's deal with this now...and our thanks will bow your food nets, I promise you."

*   *   *

The forum level of Aberuthen Warren was a proper fifty meters below surface level, carved out by hand, as many of the older warrens were, to form a vast chamber with supporting native rock pillars which soared thirty meters up to the vaulted roof.

And everywhere, there were shrubs and trees and beds of plants, separated by honest earth beaten to smoothness by the passage of many feet. Among them were public squares with benches. At the center of the forum was the heart of it—a larger public square, surrounded by hedges and featuring a field of clover underfoot.

The sun lights were all turned to yellow orange, to signify the shift from the active nocturnal period to the sleeping period. The lowering light cast shadows across the forum.

As the members of the Collective spilled down the stairs and into the central square, the entrance was sealed against the heat, dust and dryness of the coming day.

Despite the size of the forum, people were packed into the public areas, many of them sitting or lying on the flooring. Those that were reclining wore the pale, thin coverings the Collectives preferred for their coolness, protection against ultraviolet light and the ever-present dust.

As always, whenever she stepped into a warren, Saima paused to adjust to the rich aromas that marked warren life. While she absorbed the impact of the scents and stenches, she examined the people lying and sitting on the floors and benches. "There is a second Collective here?" she asked.

"Aye, but not from any design of mine, I assure you. We're a C-classified warren," Grazia Ederne said. "And we've been at capacity for a generation."

A C Classification meant they were licensed to house three thousand people, Saima recalled.

"This here is all that is left of the Honeyherb Collective," Ederne added. She waved toward a short man in a stained and torn djellaba, with very dark features, who got to his feet and came toward them. "This is Eydís Mertens, Director of the Honeyherb Collective."

Mertens nodded grimly.

"What happened to your vehicles? Your salvage?" Brid said. "There is nothing above us but sand."

Mertens sighed. "Damn girl happened, is what."

"That's part of why we need a judge," Ederne added. "We can explain everything before him."

Brid beckoned to Markas. "Mr. Domhnall."

Out of habit, Saima and Pallas moved alongside Markas as he put himself before Governor Ederne and Director Mertens. Markas was the short step between Pallas and Saima. "Who is to be judged?" he intoned, his voice making up for the elevation he felt he lacked, despite them both assuring him it made no difference. But Markas, in private, was a gentle and sensitive man. A thoughtful one,

86

who offset Pallas' passions and drive.

Markas' ritual opening words sent a ripple over the assembled people. Those on the edges surged closer to hear everything.

Governor Ederne cleared her throat, awkwardness radiating from her. "We don't actually have the perpetrator to hand."

Markas lowered his hands, blinking. "Then how can I judge them, if they are not here to speak for themselves?"

As they swiftly learned, even if Rina Beaulau had been standing before Markas, she still would not have spoken in her own defence.

*　*　*

While Governor Ederne and Director Mertens took turns explaining to Markas what had happened, Venkat Brid spoke to Ederne's hovering assistants, coordinating the repair of the power receptor dish before the next scheduled platform transmission. Then he turned to the Collective's own team leaders and directed them to secure the caravan.

Saima heard Brid say, "Full staking, nets, wheel locks, environmental seals, the works, on every vehicle. I don't care how long it takes. There are too many unknowns surrounding us. Best to be sure."

As the team leaders hurried away to have the entrance unsealed long enough for them to climb to the surface, Saima turned her attention back to Ederne and Mertens.

Mertens was speaking. "…three days ago. A completely normal trade visit. We had close to a tonne of wiring we took from what we think was a train engine. *That* caught Ederne's eye. And her people had fresh mangoes and more. No one took any notice of the girl."

"Rina?" Markas confirmed. "She was out among your caravan?"

"Off to one side." Mertens shook his head.

Saima sensed his chagrin.

Markas looked from Mertens to Ederne. Both were uncomfortable. He asked a series of questions designed to pull the story from them, while Pallas stood with narrowed eyes, a furrow between his brows, memorizing everything to record, later.

Rina Beaulau was a deaf mute, and thirteen years old. There was more that Ederne might have said about her, most of it shadowed in her mind by a baffled frustration that was formless and told Saima nothing.

For the last year, Rina had spent as much of her active day outside as the sentries and the weather would allow. "She would stare at the sky for hours on end," Ederne added. "She was always sensitive to light levels. Noise, too. Night light seems to appeal to her. She would fight us if we tried to take her back inside before dawn, so we mostly left her alone."

When the Honeyherb Collective arrived, three days ago, Rina had stood to one side, studying the cloud formations. She had lingered outside for the two days the Collective had remained at the warren to trade and socialize. At the third sunset, the caravan had prepared to leave.

"That's when she did it," Merten said heavily. "Even as we were leaning in to get everything rolling, she zipped down the side of the caravan—fast! The girl has long legs, I give you that. She snatched Saffira's baby out of her arms, bolted through the doors of the lobby and down the steps before anyone could get their jaw re-hinged and scream protest."

Most of the Honeyherb collective had pounded after Rina and the child, with Saffira, the mother, leading them.

"Only, the warren is two kilometers across and there's five levels beneath us," Ederne said. "Rina knows every centimeter of it. She's spent her life playing in the burrows and corridors."

"You're searching for her, then?" Venkat Brid asked from just outside the tight circle of people.

"We were distracted." Mertens shifted his feet to make room for the other director. "Not long after Rina went crazy, while we were tramping through the food forests looking for her, well..." He scrubbed at his hair, bafflement and anger rolling from him in hot waves. "It had been raining. Did we mention that?"

Markas shook his head.

"Couldn't see the horizon for it sheeting down. That's

why we didn't see them coming."

Ederne cleared her throat. "Tornados," she said. "Big ones. The rainclouds hid their approach. The sentries spotted three of them touching down, less than a kilometer away, and got everyone from the Collective who wasn't already inside down the stairs, and the entrance sealed. We don't know how many tornadoes went through before the all-clear came, but as you saw for yourself, they took everything that wasn't driven into the ground, including every vehicle in Merten's caravan."

Merten sighed. "All gone..." he muttered. "And now, this."

Markas considered for a moment. "Does Rina have parents or caregivers?" he asked.

"Two parents," Ederne said.

"We will speak to them, in Rina's absence," Markas declared. Then he glanced at Saima.

She understood what he had not said. It would seem as though he was conducting the investigation, but it was she who would really be learning the truth.

*   *   *

Nari Lauge and Heleena Beaulens lived in a neat burrow running off the third level forest. The burrow had a comfortably-sized, nearly-round common room in the center and several rooms coming off it. Saima spotted through hand-smoothed archways beds with patchwork quilts and fluffed up pillows, braided rag rugs on the floors and hand-worked fabric art hiding the rocky walls.

There were no sunlights in here, with their chemical bases and photoreceptor connectors, and their hot reflector shields. Instead, there were candles and lamps making the main room glow with welcoming warmth. The rug over the earth floor was a richly patterned tapestry made of teased and dyed fibres.

"I made the rug from the bamboo I grow," Nari Lauge told Saima with a small smile. "I work in the bamboo farm." But her smile didn't shift the worry gnawing at the back of her mind.

"It's lovely," Saima said, for it was.

Heleena took her wife's hand.

Markas sat on the only remaining chair. Saima and

Pallas stood behind him.

"You are here about Rina, yes?" Heleena asked.

Markas nodded. "As Rina is not here to speak for herself, I would learn what I can from you."

But Saima was already learning, for when Markas nodded, the minds of both women tightened. Worry remained, but fear, frustration, and an exhausted resignation touched them.

They didn't know where Rina was, either. They didn't know why she had done this.

"Rina is...a difficult child," Nari said softly.

"She has challenges," Heleena added, with stout loyalty.

Tantrums. Toys used as missiles. A small child with her mouth open in a scream she couldn't voice.

"You've raised her to be a productive member of the warren, though," Markas presumed.

"She likes weeding," Nari said. "And the sunlights on her back."

Saima saw the chaotic childhood years drift into a more peaceful co-existence in the mothers' minds. A girl, taller now, her body showing signs of the woman she would become very soon, crouched among the harvest crops, her hands spreading compost, pulling weeds.

And a conflicting image. Rina standing out upon the open earth beyond the lobby, staring up at the clouds.

"She changed, just in the last year," Saima said.

The women looked up at Saima, startled.

Markas just smiled.

"You...you're an angel, aren't you?" Nari asked diffidently. "Your height..."

"Yes, I was born and raised on a platform," Saima admitted.

"And are you a registered asset, too?" Heleena asked. "You knew, just then, about Rina."

"I have some talents," Saima admitted. "But I am not registered, no."

Pallas squeezed her hand, behind Markas' back, as if he was the empath and sometimes-telepath, instead of her, and had read her distress at having to speak about her past.

Neither woman noticed, though. Nira leaned toward her. "Why would you leave the platform? It must be such a wonderful life, up there above the clouds."

Saima swallowed. Made herself speak. "Compared to living next to a forest, with all the food one wants to hand?" She shook her head.

Neither of them believed her prevarication. She could see it in their eyes. But Saima had never spoken to anyone but her husbands about why she had left her life on the platform and descended to ground level to live with the Collective.

Finding oneself at the end of a long genetic cultivation line, only to be found sterile and unable to continue the line, was not something to share with strangers. She had left that life behind, along with her many siblings and their offspring, with their prized genetics and resulting talents.

Saima cleared her throat. "Tell me what happened to Rina. About a year ago."

The two mothers looked at each other. Sorrow touched them.

"A year ago, our second daughter died," Heleena said. Her grip on Nari's hand grew firmer. "We thought at first that Rina hadn't noticed. But then she would wander outside and stay out, for all the hours of the night."

"One of the sentries always kept an eye on her," Nari added hastily. "We knew where she was."

"She just wouldn't come inside," Heleena finished.

"How did your other daughter die?" Markas asked.

"An infection...a disease. We don't know," Nari said.

The sorrow swamped them again. Guilt, too. But no matter the circumstances, parents always felt guilt. Saima ignored the sharp, biting note in their mind-voices.

"The warren doesn't have a diagnostician?" Markas asked. "There are many of them, these days."

"The Warren hasn't been able to attract one," Nari replied, her voice low.

The new diagnosticians were a sought-after asset. Most people assumed they could "see" inside an ailing patient and tell what was wrong with them that way. From the mind of the Collective's diagnostician, Saima had learned their skills were more complicated than that. They read minutiae about their patient. The angle of a squirm, the cadence of a groan. The tinge of pheromones, the odor of exhalation. Heat spots on the body. The taste of sweat and saliva and body salts. From such details, an accurate diagnosis could be made, without any of the hospitals' worth of equipment the Hedonistic Era had found necessary.

Saima stirred, the mothers' keening sorrow over the loss of their second child digging into her own chest. "Is one of those rooms Rina's?" she asked, pointing at the open archways.

Nari got to her feet and picked up a candle. "That room, there." She crossed the room toward the arch at the back, farthest from the front door. Saima followed.

Behind her, Heleena said to Markas, "You will judge my daughter fairly?"

"Everyone, no matter who they are or where they are from, has a right and a responsibility to have their actions judged fairly," Markas said, quoting directly from the Magisterial Handbook.

Saima passed into the narrow room beyond as Nari put the candle on a shelf high enough that she had to stretch to reach it. The shelf, Saima guessed, had been mounted there so candles and lanterns would be out of Rina's reach.

Saima studied the room. The bed was narrow, but looked comfortable, and was piled high with cushions and pillows in various colours. The coverlet was straightened.

There was no other furniture. From the women's' minds, Saima had caught an image of a chair smashed against the rock wall and splintering into long, dangerous shards.

An attempt had been made to smooth out the native rock, so it was a flat wall, but there were bumps and irregularities in the brown rockface. A bamboo tapestry covered the center of the longest wall, opposite the bed. It showed a Hedonistic Era house with a garden right out in the open air, with the sun in a cloudless blue sky beaming benevolently upon everything.

Where the wall met the floor, along all the walls not

covered by the bed, books were piled up upon each other, all of the piles nearly the same height, about thirty centimeters each. The books were turned so the aged, yellowed edges of the pages showed, instead of the spines.

"Rina can read?" Saima asked. The skill it must have taken to teach the girl that!

"It was too difficult to educate Rina beyond the most basic social skills," Nari said, her voice husky.

"The books…?"

"She likes to use them as toys. Building blocks," Nari replied. "We acquire any books no one else wants, just to add to her collection."

Saima stepped back so she could take in all the piles of books at once, and saw the pattern. The books had been arranged so the discolouration of the page edges ranged in a spectrum from darkest to lightest.

Such subtle perception in colour!

"I think they were more than blocks," Saima said. She bent, picked up the first pile and flipped open each dry, cracking fibre-plus cover to read the title page. The collection was a hodgepodge of esoteric knowledge. Bee-keeping. Astronomical physics. Nursery rhymes—that one was hand-written, as the less popular books often were. Orbital mechanics. Fairy tales—also written, and by the same hand, too. A copy of *The Hubris of the Hedonists*, which must surely be the most commonly printed book, anywhere. Nari and Heleena really had picked up books no one else wanted.

Saima paused when she came to the last books in the last pile, closest to the bed. She stared at the title.

Simple Sign Language for Beginners.

Her heart thudded. She looked up at Nari. "You taught her sign language?"

"What's sign language?" Nari asked.

From outside the burrow, shouting sounding. Then the sound of an air siren winding up to full volume shrieked through the forest, making Saima wince.

"Outside! An emergency outside!" Nari cried, over the siren.

The caravan was outside.

Saima dropped the books and ran.

* * *

The seal over the entrance had been thrust aside by the time Saima, Pallas and Markas reached it. People ran up the steps into the blazing light and heat of full day. Saima pulled her hood over her head and hooked her veil closed. From the corner of her eye she saw Pallas and Markas and the other Collective members climbing the steps were doing the same. It was a reflex, ingrained from years of living upon the sand.

Around the front of the steps, people hammered rusty sheets of tin, corrugated steel and planks of old, precious dressed wood into the ground, forming a circle around the steps. The materials were being pulled off the Collective's salvage carts.

"What's happening?" Saima shouted to be heard over the cries of others, as they directed each other in their efforts.

Janzen, one of the Collective, shouted back at her. "The storm that brought the tornadoes yesterday—it rained farther up the valley and the water is heading this way. A big wave of it. Meters high, they say! The platform over us sent a laser beam message. We only got it when the power dish was aligned, a couple of minutes ago!"

Saima turned to Markas and Pallas. "Our wagon!"

All three of them ran for the painted, old-fashioned wagon that was their home. Saima pressed her hand against the door, for the security team had sealed it as the Director had instructed. The interior was safe, but... "They said *meters* high!" she told Pallas and Markas.

"The platform's doppler might be wrong," Markas said calmly, although his throat worked. "The cloud might be too thick beneath them."

Pallas turned as the shouting around the entrance to the warren grew louder and the alarmed notes climbed.

"Water! Water!"

"Here it comes!"

They whirled and moved to one side of the wagon to see down the length of the caravan parked before the warren entrance. The water *was* coming—a dirty yellow wave less than knee-height. But behind it, more water frothed and rolled, carrying everything in its path.

94

"Up! Climb up!" Pallas shouted, and pulled Markas over to the wagon. "Saima, hurry!"

They clambered up the exterior of the wagon, onto the roof. They held each other steady on the mildly convex roof, watching the water approach with thudding hearts.

Everyone around the warren entrance climbed over the barrier now in place and hurried down the stairs, while a few of the Collective members copied Saima and her husbands, and climbed onto the roof of carts.

None of them had allowed for the power and fury of the water wall. It rammed up against the solid back wall of the entrance, then curled around the edges, sucking at the temporary barrier in front of the steps themselves, sliding through in places where the edges were not watertight.

The water ran beneath the front carts of the caravan, swirling around the wheels, then swiftly built up until it was pushing against the carts themselves. Venkat Brid's wagon, the front one, lurched and began to turn in the current swirling around it.

"We'll be swept away!" Pallas cried, as the water washed around the high wheels of their own wagon.

"The current can't last forever!" Markas shouted back. "Wherever we end up, we can haul the wagon back here."

Pallas pointed to the front of the caravan, where Venkat Brid's wagon slowly toppled to one side and spun around. It made sickly bubbling sounds as the water rushed into apertures and micro spaces, pouring inside the vehicle.

The Collective members straddling the roofs of carts behind Brid's watched with alarm as the overturned vehicle floated toward them, and their own carts began to spin.

Markas slapped Pallas' shoulder. "Up!!" He pointed up.

They all looked up.

A platform dirigible was floating down toward them.

Saima clapped a hand over her mouth, holding in her cry of surprise. Never had she thought the site of a dirigible would fill her with such happiness, not after she had stepped off what she thought was her last.

The oversized oval nitrogen-mix-filled balloon with its

passenger compartment hanging from beneath it was supposed to be a near replica of ancient Hedonist dirigibles used before fixed-wing technology ran rampant around the world. It had once bothered her greatly that humans were copying the Hedonists in even an innocent and approved technology, but it allowed platform people to reach the ground to trade their services for warren-grown food.

Platforms sent the solar energy they collected from above the dense cloud cover to warren and collective receiver dishes via laser, to run the few approved machines and the limited permitted technology, including the receiving dishes themselves. The platforms dispersed the high-altitude cloud which warmed the atmosphere, while helping preserve the lower level, dense cloud cover that helped cool the shattered, desolate earth that remained once the Hedonists had finished destroying it.

The dirigible was descending nose-on to their position on the roof of the wagon. Saima couldn't see the insignia on the tail end of the balloon, but the lateral fans were working, bringing the tail around, so the flank of the ship and the steps into the cabin faced them.

She saw the tail fans. Above them, the stylized "R". It was the *Rasathamon*.

Pallas pulled her against him. "It's just the dirigible. Your family won't be on it."

Saima nodded, her throat working.

The steps up into the cabin were extended and the pilot brought the dirigible down in tiny increments. Even then, the wagon shifted beneath them, preparing to lurch and slide away.

The pilot repositioned the airship, while a crew member hung from the open door, his helmet off, and a hand extended. His face was not familiar to her, and he was short. Warren or Collective-born, then, and a new arrival upon the *Rasathamon* platform.

By unspoken assent, Saima and Pallas hoisted Markas between them up onto the bottom step. The crew member hauled Markas inside. Then Saima, then Pallas.

Saima moved along the cabin, stripping aside her veil and hood, for the air in airships was pure, scrubbed of all impurities. She clutched the high corners of the seats, fighting for calm, as the big airship rose gracefully into the air and hovered. She bent and peered through the windows, down at the water-washed caravan and the roughly protected opening of the warren entrance.

Everywhere across the valley, even licking up along the low sides of the featureless trough, was dirty water. The caravan's vehicles floated down the valley, spinning and lurching as their wheels caught at the earth beneath. The taller, top-heavy carts had tipped onto their sides just as Brid's had done.

The airship moved forward, matching the speed of the floating carts, then drifted downward to pick up the remaining Collective members on the other roofs.

Saima turned to the helmet-less crew member. "You came down because you saw the water wave heading this way?"

He nodded, his gaze raking over her face. Her height. He'd recognized her, for not only did her family have remarkable genes, they also had remarkably similar facial features.

"I need you to take a message back to the platform," she told the crew member.

*   *   *

It took two hours for the water to subside enough to allow them to wade through ankle-deep gritty puddles to the warren entrance. They had to return to the warren, for Brid was there and their wagons were at the end of the valley. It might take days, yet, for the engineers in the Collective to retrieve the wagons and pronounce them fit for travel.

Besides, Saima had unfinished business in the warren.

She climbed down the damp steps to the forum level and shook off her hood and veil. Everyone in the forum was on their feet, talking in high voices and gesturing, despite the late hour. Saima made her way to the square in the middle, where she knew she would find Brid and Merten and Governor Ederne.

They were at the heart of the hubbub, as she had expected, already discussing recovery strategies and rebuilding. The parcelling out of resources. Soon, the

97

captain of the *Rasathamon,* Kjell Monti, would arrive to tower over them and learn how he might assist.

Somehow, she had to pull their attention away from their natural priorities.

A murmur started at the back of the forum, leaping forward in waves. Through a gap in the hedges which surrounded the central square with its bright green clover carpet, Saima glimpsed a tight knot of people, moving closer.

The group emerged into the square and spread out, revealing a tall, slender Warren-woman, holding a one-year-old infant in her arms, bouncing the child on her hip the way mothers did. The child looked up at her with trusting eyes.

Saima recognized the girl from the images she'd seen in her mothers' minds.

Rina Beaulau.

That she be here, right now, fit into Saima's expectations. After living with Pallas and Markas for ten years, she had grown accustomed to thinking in patterns herself.

A woman in Collective whites pushed forward, a wordless cry of relief emerging. She snatched the child from Rina's arms. Rina didn't try to keep the child—also part of the pattern.

The woman kissed her child and hugged it, then dropped to the clover and put the child on her lap and inspected every inch of the infant.

Rina simply watched, while everyone shouted at her, demanding explanations.

The mother looked up, her expression bewildered. "But, she is dry. Clean! The moss is fresh…!"

The baby reached up and patted its mother's cheek, enjoying her astonishment and light tones.

Markas nudged Saima's arm. He moved his head, a tiny shift. *Speak to her.*

Saima edged through and around the swirl of concerned people. They stood closer and tighter around Rina, but Saima squeezed between them until she stood directly in front of the girl. She smiled at Rina.

A tiny furrow pushed the girl's brows together.

Puzzlement. Saima wasn't behaving as expected.

Saima put her arms together, as she would if she held a child. Rocked her arms.

Rina stared at her steadily, not reacting.

But her mind spoke volumes.

"She learned how to care for her sister, when her sister was a baby," Saima called.

That brought silence around them, as people processed Saima's statement.

"That is true!" a woman called.

Saima straightened to look over everyone's heads, not surprised to see Nari and Heleena making their way through the crowd to reach their daughter.

Saima bent to look directly into Rina's eyes. She touched the girl's cheek, to get her attention, for Rina's gaze said her thoughts were far away.

Rina looked back at Saima.

Saima pointed upward, several times. Looked up. And listened. Hard.

Images poured in, astonishing her.

Saima straightened again. "Rina can read the weather!" she declared. "She knew the tornados were coming! She took the child to make everyone chase her down into the warren and into safety!"

Silence, dressed with gasps of shock.

Rina peered up at Saima, rocking slightly from side to side. She laughed—a silent motion that showed her joy at being understood.

Governor Ederne and Rina's mothers gathered around Saima. "You can understand her?" Heleena asked, her tone one of desperate hope.

"Not exactly, but I know someone who does. He's on his way down here from the *Rasathamon* right now," Saima told them.

"Who is that?" Pallas asked softly from just behind her. He was protecting her back.

Saima turned to him. "My brother, Nigul. He's deaf— he stood too close to the platform blades when he was a child. But he knows sign language, and how to read and write." She turned to Rina. "And so does Rina."

*   *   *

It astonished Saima how old Nigul had grown since she had left the platform, even though the same age markers must surely line her own face.

He sat on one of the benches in the public square, surrounded by the leaders: Brid, Ederne, Mertens and Captain Monti, who was a third generation angel and stood more than two meters tall, thanks to the lower gravity in the upper atmosphere. Nari and Heleena were also part of the group, and Markas, with Pallas beside him in his recording role.

Beside Nigul, Rina sat cross-legged, her head down, rocking gently.

Nigul spoke, his words distorted by his inability to hear his own pronunciations. "Rina *can* see the weather," he explained. "That is why she watches the clouds whenever she can. She is also listening to the wind, tasting the air, the static, the temperature...there are many other details that she notices—far more than other humans."

"She had always been sensitive to touch and sound and light," Nari murmured.

Nigul watched Nari's mouth, then said, "But she only really put it together about a year ago."

Nari nodded. "When her sister died."

"No," Saima said. "There was another event that happened at that time, that triggered her talent."

"Menarche," Ederne said, sounding winded.

Saima nodded. "Assets often learn of their talents at puberty." She turned to Nigul. "She knew the water was coming, too, didn't she? She only emerged with the child after the water had gone."

Nigul nodded, his gaze on her mouth. "She didn't know your Collective was here. She was worried about the Honeyherb Collective, for they wanted to leave and the tornado storm was coming...and the storm water after it, for there is nothing at the top end of the valley to halt the water."

Pallas broke the silence he usually observed while in secretary mode. "And what does she see coming next?" His tone was urgent. But Nigul wouldn't hear that.

Nigul turned to Rina and tapped her shoulder.

She looked up at him with a smile, her head still

tilted. He signed at her, a rapid fluttering of his hands.

Rina moved her hands more slowly, but in a similar way.

Nigul looked around the group. "Nothing like the storm. Nights of calm. Days of heat and dust. For a very long time."

Pallas nodded, as if Nigul had confirmed something he expected.

Ederne made a soft sound. "I've never seen Rina so... responsive, before." She pressed her hands together. "We cannot provide for her here," she said sadly. "We don't have the skills. The knowledge."

"It can be learned," Nigul assured her.

"I think that now we can talk to her," Markas said, "that we might ask Rina herself what she would like to do."

* * *

It took nearly ten days for the carts and wagons of the Winterwillow Collective to be retrieved and repaired, ready to continue on their nomadic way. In that time, a great many decisions were made. Some members of the Collective had chosen to stay in the warren, while members of the Honeyherb Collective joined the Winterwillow Collective. Yet more would be travelling with the Collective to new warrens, or to join collectives they came across on their journeys.

Saima spent time with Nigul, learning her family's news and affairs, but refused politely when he suggested she visit the platform herself.

At sunset on the tenth day, everyone emerged from the warren, to say goodbye to the Collective.

The valley was completely dry, once more. The dust rose with every bootstep, to clog noses and irritate eyes. The Collective members fastened their veils quickly.

Saima bent and showed Rina how to tuck her veil loop behind her ear.

Rina tugged at the cloth over her nose, her eyes dancing.

"Yes, you're a Collector, now," Saima assured her. She awkwardly made the sign for *pretty*.

Rina tugged at the white djellaba that Saima had shortened for her, then ran and skipped, spun around and

101

ran back. Saima couldn't help laughing, for joy was bubbling through Rina's mind. She was going to be *outside* and could stay outside forever!

Heleena and Nari, who stood beside Pallas and Markas, also laughed, but with tears in their eyes.

"Line up! Forward, ho!" the whipmaster called.

"Quickly, say goodbye," Saima told Rina, catching her arm and pointing to her mothers.

Nari and Heleena rushed forward to hug their daughter and kiss her cheeks.

Pallas and Markas picked up their wagon yoke and leaned against the bars, putting all their weight against them to get the wagon moving.

Saima turned to Nari and Heleena. "Rina will be taught to read and write. And her talents plumbed. I promise you." It wasn't the first time she had made the fervent promise in the last ten days.

"We know," Heleena, the calmer of the two said, her tone resigned. "She will thrive, with you. And we will see her when Winterwillow visits—Director Brid says he will return."

Saima caught Rina's hand and drew her forward, to keep pace with the wagon, which was finally moving. Pallas and Markas relaxed, one hand on the yoke bars, for once the wagon was underway, little effort was needed to keep it rolling. Later, Saima would take their place. Eventually Rina would need to learn how, too.

But that was for later.

They waved goodbye to the Warren-folk until they could no longer see them.

Rina tugged on Saima's hand, which she was still holding.

Saima looking down at her, with a smile.

Rina pulled something out of her pocket and lifted it up to Saima. It was the book of sign language.

Saima laughed and nodded as she took the book. "I *will* learn," she promised.

"We all will," Pallas said.

Rina tilted her head, as if she was listening to Pallas. In Rina's mind, Saima read happy understanding. Rina knew the gift had been accepted.

The girl turned and ran, her long legs stretching out.

"Don't go too far!" Saima called uselessly after her.

"She won't," Markas told her. "And the others will watch out for her, too."

They walked companionably for a while. Travelling days were also deep conversation and deep thinking days. Time for learning and exchanging ideas. Before them and behind them, the owners of the other carts and wagons and their drivers all chatted, while their vehicles rolled along the flat, parched earth.

"Pallas, why did you ask Rina what she could see of the weather in the future?" Saima said, after a while.

Markas looked at his husband, his brow lifted. He wanted to know that answer, too.

Pallas shrugged, both hands on the yoke bar. "I wanted to know how far ahead she could predict the weather. The Hedonists were uniformly bad at measuring weather more than a few days into the future."

Silence fell once more.

"I don't think that was the only reason you asked," Markas said.

Pallas' silence extended. Neither of them rushed to prod him into answering. The silence would goad him into it. Pallas didn't like to leave questions unanswered.

"What do you see in Rina's mind, when you stand with her and stare at the clouds, Saima?" Pallas asked.

"Nothing," Saima said. "Nights of stillness, days of heat and dust. Just like she told Nigul."

"It's getting worse, isn't it?" Markas said softly. "Not better, the way everyone hopes." He added bitterly. "The Great Hope of Humanity."

The great hope to live above ground once more, under open blue sky and a friendly yellow sun, like in the tapestry on Rina's bedroom wall in the warren.

"Pallas, you spent all that time reading the books in the warren, all their latest archives and datasets," Saima said. "Did you learn something from that? Is a new pattern emerging?"

Pallas made a soft sound, deep in his throat. "It filled in a hole in the data I have already," he admitted. "I'm glad we'll be going back to Aberuthen in the future. I saw that the heat, the dust, the unpredictable weather...it will be with us for a while yet. But..." He paused.

Markas slapped his shoulder. "You're *teasing*."

"I'm really not," Pallas said gently. "I'm starting to see something emerge from the data, as if I can see it from the corner of my eye."

"Or smell it in the clouds?" Saima asked.

Pallas nodded. "Something is coming. Something new. And I think...something better."

Rina ran back to the wagon and picked up Saima's hand.

The two men pushed the wagon and the new family moved onward

This story first appeared in Knotted Road Press's *Blaze Ward Presents #7: Every Tomorrow Worse?*

The Portal on the Third Day
Tyree Campbell

on the third day the portal closed
between your world and mine
like a camera lens
your glistening eyes
longing . . .

Who?

Sharmon Gazaway is a Dwarf Stars Award finalist. Her fiction is featured in New Myths' Best Of anthology, Cosmic Muse, and in The Best of MetaStellar Year Two. Her work appears in Solarpunk Magazine, The Forge Literary Magazine, ParABnormal, The Fairy Tale Magazine, and in various anthologies. Sharmon writes from the Deep South where she lives beside a historic cemetery haunted by the wild cries of pileated woodpeckers. Instagram @sharmongazaway.

Kylie Wang is a Taiwanese writer who grew up in Hong Kong and is now a high school student in California. Her short works have received 30+ awards and publications, including from YoungArts, the Scholastics Arts and Writing Award, Paper Lanterns, and Bluefire. Her co-authored Young Adult novel, "Stuck in Her Head," is coming out with Earnshaw Books in October. You can find her on Instagram @kyliewangwrites.

Cameron Cooper says: I am a full-time fiction author, with 35 traditionally published novels, and over 200 indie titles. Under my Cameron Cooper pen name, my space opera novel, *Hammer and Crucible*, came fourth in Hugh Howey's

Self-Published Science Fiction Contest #2. I write fantasy under Taylen Carver, and women's fiction under my name. I am an Australian Canadian, and a member of SFWA.

Born in Cuba, **Matias Travieso-Diaz** migrated to the United States as a young man. He became an engineer and lawyer and practiced for nearly fifty years. After retirement, he took up creative writing. Eighty of his short stories have been published or accepted for publication in anthologies and paying magazines, blogs, audio books and podcasts. Some of his unpublished works have also received "honorable mentions" from several paying publications. A first collection of his stories, "The Satchel and Other Terrors" has recently been released and is available on Amazon and other book outlets.

Terrie Leigh Relf is a college instructor, life coach, editor, and published writer. She handles *The Hungur Chronicles*, a biannual digest of vampires in outer space, and runs the drabble contest for Hiraeth Publishing. Her latest novel is *Sisterhood of the Blood Moon*, which can be purchased from the Shop at www.hiraethsffh.com; her latest poetry collection, *Postcards From Space*, can also be bought there.

Tyree Campbell is an award-winning storyteller with a considerable resume of science fiction and fantasy novels, novellas, and short stories. He writes the Bombay Sapphire superheroine series for Pro Se Press. His latest novel, *Gallium Girl*, features an unlikely trio of vampire, werewolf, and human woman in search of a future. All his work is available from the Shop at www.hiraethsffh.com, primarily because he runs the place.